THE CRAZY
HUNTER

THE NEW DIRECTIONS

KAY BOYLE
THE CRAZY HUNTER

RONALD FIRBANK
CAPRICE

HENRY MILLER
A DEVIL IN PARADISE

DYLAN THOMAS
EIGHT STORIES

TENNESSEE WILLIAMS
THE ROMAN SPRING
OF MRS. STONE

KAY BOYLE

THE CRAZY HUNTER

A NEW DIRECTIONS

The Crazy Hunter is also available in the New Directions Revived
Modern Classic edition of Kay Boyle's Three Short Novels: The Crazy
Hunter, The Bridegroom's Body, and Decision.

Manufactured in the United States of America.
New Directions Books are printed on acid-free paper.
First published as a New Directions Bibelot in 1993.
Published simultaneously in Canada by Penguin Books Canada
Limited.

Library of Congress Cataloging-in-Publication Data

Boyle, Kay, 1902-92
    The crazy hunter / Kay Boyle
        p.   cm.
    ISBN 0-8112-1233-5 (alk. paper)
    1. Family–England–Fiction. 2. Horses–Fiction. I. Title.
PS3503.09357C73 1993
813' .54–dc20

                                        93-8246
                                          CIP

New Directions Books are published for James Laughlin
by New Directions Publishing Corporation,
80 Eighth Avenue, New York 10011

THE CRAZY
HUNTER

Chapter One

THE WOMAN and the girl began undressing in the bushes near the water, modestly taking their garments off at a little distance from each other and with their backs turned so as not to surprise each other's abashed flesh. The sun came thin but warm through the just opening buds and the tight flickering leaves of the branches, dappling the two lowered faces and the bared arms and legs with shadow. The girl had ripped her jersey over her head and flung it aside and kicked her sandals off; the tweed skirt lay discarded behind her on the earth beneath the burgeoning spring-like twigs. When she had pulled the tight blue woolen swimming suit up over her belly and breasts, she straightened up and came out onto the bank, buttoning one strap over the shoulder still, and stood there looking: the white naked legs drawn close together, slender and the flesh delicate as southern dogwood flowers, the head held straight upon the round slender neck, the temples hollow and bare with the black hair drawn back above the ears and falling almost to the shoulders. The hair and the skin's untroubled purity, and the wide, up-tilted, the seemingly drugged or glazed transparent eyes gave her a look un-English as the Orient. And now the woman in her bathing-dress came stooping out, picking her own clothes up carefully and folding them over and laying them in order on the meadow grass above the wall of sedges that grew from the running water.

3

"Fold your things up, Nan," the woman said. "Pick your clothes up and put them somewhere all together so you'll know where they are when you get out," saying it not so much from will or habit as from the need to stop quickly this or any gap of silence between them. The arms, like the body in the black skirted bathing-dress, were full, powder-white, unblemished: these (with the forebone long and prominent in them, despite their unstained beauty, and the flesh gone slack), and the thickening, sloping shoulders and the neck's yoke signs of the consummation between flesh and time. From now on was the decline, the deterioration towards age, to come. Only the hands, reaching for the plaid blouse to smooth it out and fold it, and the face and the narrow feet in the black tennis shoes, were part still of a thinner, shyer woman's corporeity: perhaps one who had never entered into marriage willingly or given birth but who remained still tentative, still virgin, still unformed. "Nan, pick up your clothes before you go in," she said, the slow, still-innocent eyes searching the ground itself for flaw, saying it hopelessly into youth's deafness and imperviousness.

But the cold was on the girl's feet already, the water rising slowly on the pure legs as she slid down the bank's edge to the stream: the blurred face lowered, part in ecstasy, part fear, to watch the thin silver line of cold pass the ankles and mount the flesh to the knees and pass them, rising, until it had clasped her waist, her breasts, her throat, and for an instant twisted her shocked face in consternation. Then her arms began moving and she was swimming against the pouring current, the teeth shaking in her head with cold. So the last time I did this I was fifteen, two years

4

back, she began thinking quickly against the rushing slabs of water. I hadn't been away yet and I wasn't afraid. I didn't know what it was yet. Now I can feel everything stopping, the heart, the blood, the muscles hardening as if I were working my way through ice and becoming ice and the land and sky congealing tight around me. But the mother standing on her big bare legs on the grass saw the sun falling on the soft short hair that mounted black against the current, and the girl's slim arms falling and rising, the shoulders and the bent arms as they fell chalk-white in motion through the dark water, thrusting it down behind her with small quick strokes like someone quickly mounting a steep ladder or jerking up a greased pole at a country fair.

"How is it, Nan?" she called out. "Cold?" And now her own body slumped over and broke through the sedge and the reed-sweet into the stream's fast deep bed. For a moment she swam strongly, without gasping and her chin high, and then she turned lazily onto her back and rode there, the blue rubber cap edging the longish, pale face, the big arms thrashing backwards. "Warm," she called peacefully across the water's rapid murmuring. "Just the first plunge that takes your breath off. . . ."

The way home takes it from you and doesn't return it, the girl was saying, because every year of youth is still there in the furniture and the rugs and the marks on the glass. There is a school of children everywhere with me here, all of them that one child I was once running along the house's east ivy-covered wall and down through the stables and pastures; home putting short skirts on me and picture-books on the shelves in my room. The child who

5

scratched that drawing with a nursery pin on the inside of the banisters above the sixth bar on the first flight is still your bone, your skin, your muscle of the eye, your nail and tooth, the same physically projected child that dies now in the water's ice. She let the current turn and draw her down-stream towards the blue rubber cap, past the water-beaded floating head with its face turned upward in repose to the sun's light hanging palely on the meadows and trees.

"I'm not so good as I used to be," Nan said. "I'm going to get out, mother. I've forgotten how to swim in cold water after swimming over there."

"Climbing mountains ought to give you wind enough," the woman said, floating quietly with the stream. She lay vast, wide, bloated-seeming, her arms and legs dangling swollen under water.

"Sometimes when you learn one thing you forget another," Nan said, her teeth knocking in her mouth again. She reached up for the willow's roots and pulled herself, straining, out of the water. "I spoke German until I learned French, and in Italy I forgot everything I knew in French." On her hands and knees she sought under the bushes for the towel, tossed the tweed skirt and the jersey aside on the fresh, glinting earth, saying: "One year I know algebra and another year geometry. I never know them both the same winter." In a moment she turned on her knees and came back to the bank and sat there hunched in the towel, shaking, her toe-nails showing bluish at the edge. "Or when I get halfway good in charcoal drawing I forget how to work with oils, and the year I took architectural design I couldn't do life-class afterwards." She started drying her hair at the back with her hand inside the towel, shaking the soft dark locks loose. "And it's the same thing if I admire things," she said, stopping to pick a blade of pressed grass from her knee inside the towel's shade. "When I was so keen on the Renaissance I couldn't—"

"You're tucked up, that's what it is," said the woman smartly from the water, churning backwards with her arms. "You're still growing, you know, and you've been wearing yourself out with all this studying. Yesterday I saw one thing," she said, drifting wide and peaceful. "You haven't forgot how to ride a horse."

Nor have I forgotten to breathe or speak my native tongue, only how to walk into the house and through its rooms as if I belonged there any longer, or swim in water that knew me young, or sit under this tree that knew my legs climbing up it once, or how to look at her and talk to her because she is still talking Then and I am ahead in what there will be for me or in Now. I am home now, this is home, and there is no place for me because every place is taken by that child who will not die.

"I don't think I'm still growing," she said. "Anyway, my feet aren't growing. I've worn the same size shoes for two years now. I got my navy suède brogues to wear on my fifteenth birthday to go to Pellton to Mary's lunch party, and I can still wear them without them hurting."

"Look at your riding-breeches!" said the mother, floating near the sedges. "You've shot up four inches at least since September. That's why I don't want to get you a top-price twill. You'll be out of it in six months. It isn't worth it."

"Yes," she said, "yes," almost in pain, and then as if that was the end of it she sat without speaking, rubbing

7

the damp hair off her neck with her hand inside the towel. Mother, I know my bones, I live in this flesh, I know I have stopped growing. Look at me, I am another woman sitting up here on the grass, only not established, not recognized yet, but I am a woman sitting here watching you refuse the stream its current by your will. Just let me say this and say without looking at you that I've been three days, no, three nights and two days back and I can't stay. It's June, but it's just spring here because things are late this year. That's why the water is cold and the buds hardly open and the sedges the way rushes are in May usually, everything a month or more than that behind the season. But in other countries, in southern countries, things would be different now: the roses out strong and hot and sweet in the gardens, and the students, poets, painters coming back to their rooms along the river not looking like other people, their eyes different, and their voices not like other people's, and their shoes older, and their heads bare the way mine was bare all winter through the galleries and in the art museums and even in the churches, for even in Italy they don't seem to care if you put a handkerchief over your hair in respect any more. You walk in at noon out of the hot streets and the sun and your blood is consecrated, it becomes cool and pious with the devout pace of your feet across the stones, and you kneel down under the rising pillars in the granite dark, believing, believing. It is not religion, or Catholicism, or the belief of the Church of England, but it is your spirit on its knees at last just learning the words for its articulation. Students, she did not say aloud but sat silent rubbing her cold breasts dry beneath the towel, their faces looking different from other

8

faces because they are still on the adventure, looking for a thing nobody here wants or has heard of wanting: knowledge or the way to knowledge or else simply the way, because of what families or convention want, of keeping curious and keeping free. All last winter I wore my clothes the way they did, as if I were a student instead of just making the pretense at it, and walked like that, and now she watched her mother emerge from the water, draw herself out by the feminine thinnish hand which seized the damp rope of the tree's uncovered root. The stuff of the wet bathing-skirt shaped the firm muscles in the thighs that gripped toward land, and in some hopeless and unreclaimed contrition, the girl stretched her own bare arm out from the towel and saw the goose-flesh powdering her skin whitely to the wrist as her arm stiffened to aid the other woman up the bank. When their fingers met and clasped, the girl's face flashed suddenly up, fervent, humble, eager, but now the mother burst out laughing, slipping and scrambling there on her broad knees in the mud; either knowing what was to come or else not knowing quite and fearful of what the words might be, she pulled herself finally up laughing onto the grass and ripped the blue rubber casing from her head and shook out her short graying curled hair and glanced quickly across the sky.

"Well, the sun's thinning out all right, Nan. Your hand's as cold as charity," she said, the voice light, inconsequential, speaking merely for the sake of sound. "You're foolish not to have taken your suit right off as soon as you were out. It chills you sitting in it like that." She was moving off, rump-high, groping on wet hands and knees to the pile of folded clothing. "Come along. We'll get our things on and run up to the paddocks," she said.

It was she who led the way along the foot-worn, cattle- and man-marked path that ran between the wild hedge and the rushes in the water, and the daughter followed, listening to the talk which led up to money now and stopped short there. The price of the seventh brood-mare, and the stud fees; on went the mother's voice ahead, talking of buying wider pasture while the big arm and the bathing-bag swung at the foxtails as she passed. Nan came over the pressed grass of the walk behind her, her feet in sandals, the vague, dream-drugged, rapt eyes watching the weeds and the branches move in the sun while the water slid off through the fields and the woman's voice went on before her:

"There's no worse business than this kind of thing we have to do, growing horses on the same ground year after year. I keep racking my brains for some way out of it and how to get hold of another set of paddocks to make use of alternate years like a rich man's stud where money is no object. There's the saying that a sheep's foot is golden and that's what has saved the ground from going horse-proud." The voice went quickly, ceaselessly on, faintly contentious, acrimonious, in the drifting light of afternoon. The back of her neck stood broad and thickening beneath her sailor hat and the cropped hairs lay, wet from swimming, flat against the dust-white skin. "Putting cattle on and off the paddocks, in and out while the stud is going on, it's a heartbreaking business. Salting the rough grasses so the cattle will eat them off or mowing the grasses off and getting the sheep in, there's no end to it." She hit out at the foxtails with her bag. "I know what I want," she said savagely, coming closer to the bitter statement of it. "If I had enough money for it. Grassland kept in good heart by resting, d' y' see, Nan? Acres of fresh rested cock's foot and rye grass and fiorin. Ah, I can see it all right in my mind's eye, but what can I do about it? Anyone knowing anything about horses would see it like this, but the one man who has anything to do with it goes using the money up in other ways—"

This was not the beginning of it or anywhere near the beginning: it was merely the high-spot of the story restated so that she could begin to tell it all over again. It had started in those letters written to the young ladies' boarding school in Florence, crossed land and water to another country and begun abruptly in the big wide Italian room with the girls' three beds in it: "Nan, I had put money aside towards buying new pasture and what did your father do but up and buy this stag-faced gelding without any rhyme or reason for doing it, except he'd had too much to drink."

He hasn't any preferences or any real will of his own, it went on in the letters or else in the voice carrying it along the cattle and dairy path ahead. He does it out of, what's the word I want, Nan, I don't mean out of spite but something almost like it only queerer, because I'm the one who has the money, born with it, kept it, doubled it after your grandfather died, and your father has to show he's somebody with something, even if it's only the say-so. He wants to prove to me and everybody else what a man he is by going out and buying an animal I haven't had a finger or an eye on, and drawing the check out to fool them into thinking any of it's his, doing it after a few drinks to show them what it's like, a man's signature and a man's bank

account. And he knows I'll stand by him; it's what he
trades on, that I won't let him down. Seven, eight years
back he spent that fortune on cattle when he knew, sober
anyway he knew, that polled cattle were the only kind
we could use with horses on the farm. He had the breed
names in his notebook when he went off to the fair: Galloways, Red Polls or Aberdeen Angus I'd put down for him,
thinking to give him the satisfaction of the responsibility.
But after whatever he had at the Ship he must have said
to himself, I'll show her. If she's British and the money's
hers, I'm Canadian and I'll have the choice and the say. I
cried a week over it after but that didn't do any good, and
the cattle once re-sold fetched half the price of what he'd
paid at the public sales, and I had to swallow that too. And
next was the unproved sire he brought home instead of a
high-class stallion, without running out its pedigree even.
Try always if you can to nick with the *sire's* dam's blood
and leave the *sire's* sire's blood as your outcross whenever
it's possible to do it, I'd told him since the beginning. I'd
written it down for him, but nothing scientific ever mat-
tered to him. If he likes the look of a thing, or if he's had
enough of someone knowing better than he does, or after
a drink or two, he'll have his head for once whatever the
price, so home he comes with this horse and there we were
with it, a practical dead-loss on our hands. But even with
it down in print before him you can't teach a Canadian
anything about a horse's predominate blood. Ah, it's been
a heart-breaking business with your father, Nan; if he
kept his hands on paints or chess sets it would be one
thing, but after he's started drinking at the sales and has
the bee in his bonnet that he knows, it would break your

heart wide open. But I've never put my foot down about the joint account and that's what I should have done from the beginning. I've always let him go on drawing on the money for the sake of his manliness, or like giving him the tail-end of a career or an occupation because he never had one of his own. And why do I keep on doing it like a fool?—only because he comes back crying over what he's done once he's seen the folly of it, crying and sorry and swearing never to do it again and ready to die for it and willing to pay back every penny out of tobacco money, and swearing to paint a picture worth more than everything he's lost. . . .

"He's only spent the money wrong like that about twice, mother," the girl said. Hatless, stockingless, she walked behind, the dream-rapt eyes watching the weeds and branches stir and quiver in the sun.

"Three times!" the woman ahead cried out. "There were the horned cattle and the worthless sire, and now this time it's this crazy hunter! He brings in this stag-faced hack at the price you'd lay out for a thoroughbred beast, and never thinking after what he'd had to drink, of having him up to pass the vet. Jolly as can be he comes in without a certificate either way, and the man who'd sold it to him out of the country so it happened. And why did your father do it? Just to show me he can get the money out of my hands when he wants! We're stocking a stud-farm, I told him, not a riding-school. But the money was already gone and the price of new paddocks shot again—"

"Was it much? Could it have been as much as that?" the girl said, the black hair back from the hollow temples, the eyes wild-violet soft and tender, the bare blue-veined feet in the sandals wandering dreamily, soundlessly on by the stream.

"Ah, no, not so much as the price of new land, no," said the mother, striking at the tall fox-grasses with her bag. "Nothing like what has been paid for horses, nothing compared to what Sir Mallaby Deeley paid for 'Solario,' for instance," she said with bitter irony. "Never forty-odd thousand pounds, of course, but still for me it was something. It was enough to put off looking at land or even thinking of new paddocks for another year or more until something has had the time to collect and stop the hole up—"

The girl started talking quietly behind her.

"Candy says he bought Brigand for me," she was saying. "He says he wants me to have Brigand to ride and do with as I please. I told Candy I didn't want to hunt any more and he said I could have him anyway for mine—if I wanted him—I mean, if I stay—"

"He's leggy," the mother said quickly, almost quick enough to stop the sound of the last words short before she would have to hear them said, and she went on talking loud and fast. "There's bad blood in him somewhere, sire or dam; he's queer. Your father picked him for his shoulders, but anyone who knows will tell you that's a luxury item. A bad horse can trick a novice time and again with pretty shoulders."

Home three days, the mother began thinking now a little wildly, and already that face as if they'd put her in prison for life, and already the words beginning to be dropped and the hints. She went along the stream's side, irritated now, hitting impatiently at the heads of the weeds, think-

ing of the girl following a little way behind her and thinking It's her good-looks that have done it. None of us
thought she'd turn out like that, and now summer's good
enough to be wasted at home but later she'll have to be
off where the remarks men on the street or men she's met
pass about her will be nourishment enough. Ah, I know
very well what it is you want, she thought slyly, and at
the same time with an impatient recognition of the slyness,
and I'm your mother and I'll keep you from it as long as
I can. It's all very fine for you but it isn't fine enough,
Nan; you're seventeen, you can very well wait till you're
twenty to know what you want and to hear the things
they'll always have to say about your face and figure.

"Your father—" she began, but suddenly, as if wakened
from the walking dream and crying out in sleep, the girl
called:

"Mother, look at that bird up there!"

Once they had been walking along here to the paddocks,
perhaps two years back it was, anyway before the board-
ing-school in Florence, and it was something else that
stopped them short like this on the path, and the mother
now, as then, turned with her bathing-bag in her hand and
the identical sailor hat (which perhaps was not the same
one from summer to summer but which might have been)
shaded her face from what was not sun or even light so
much as merely the absence of rain. I can't look, if I can't
look down there again I can't. I can't bear looking at it,
I can't look again, said Nan's voice over the two years of
almost having forgotten what its shape was and how it
lay against the bottom in the mud.

"What are you talking about, Nan?" said the mother

with no alteration in the tone or face, neither more impatient or less, saying it now exactly as she had said it then.

"Mother, look, there's a bird caught up there in the trees," the girl said, thinking: Two years ago the thing was lying in the water and I couldn't look down at it again. I stood staring at her face until she finally turned her face down to see, the hat brim lowering so that I couldn't see her eyes any more, only the nostrils whitening along the edges and her mouth opening as if to make a sound but not making it, and then she threw her bag down on the path. We'll have to get him out quick, she said. Nan, I'll go down and get him and if you can get hold of his arms from the bank while I push him from below we ought to make it. He's got his cap on still, the mother said. Mother, I can't, I can't do anything, said Nan's voice, dying. I can't. I'm too afraid.

So slowly, the act witnessed only by herself because the girl crouched on the path had covered her face with her hands, the mother turned the body over in the water, kneeling in her clothes in the stream while the water ran cold across her doubled-up legs and to her hips. It's Sykes, she said without looking up. What I thought. It's Sykes. He's dead. And slowly, breathing hard with the effort, she got him out over the rushes and up the bank alone, thought Nan, while I sat here shaking and crying and trying not to see. But still I saw, because I remember seeing his head fall backwards on his neck and hit the grass and concrete by the paddock's post and his adam's apple jerk up higher in his throat and stop there and not come down again the way a living man's would. I remember her saying He must have drowned last Saturday night (and this was Monday afternoon), dead drunk, perhaps drinking with your father. She stood up and stood looking down at him, and then she leaned over and pulled the beak of the black-and-white checkered cap he was wearing down across his face. He wasn't a good groom anyway, the mother said wiping her hands in her handkerchief. I've been thinking for two days he'd gone off dishonestly but this was honest enough, the old souse, she said.

Holding her bathing-bag now and looking off in the direction of the trees clumped at a little distance in the meadow, she said:

"Where? A bird caught? I can't see it, Nan. Where?" Because she must turn around to look for it, her back was put now to where the paddocks lay beyond the stream's next bend, masked by the drooping willows, and this was more than she had the patience left for, for she'd already got the smell of horses down the wind. "Where in the world can you possibly see a bird caught?" she said almost in irritation.

"There," the girl said, and the lifted hand was narrow and angular as a boy's hand set strangely at the white arm's extremity. "It's holding onto something in the tree there, or else it's caught by something," she said, the hand lifted, pointing, square at the fingertips and the resolute square nails cut short on a doer's not a dreamer's hand.

The trees they looked at were various and of variable green, standing high and lovely now against the misting heavens, their pale and dark, strong and fanciful greens shaking and beckoning in a breeze that did not touch the woman's or the girl's lifted face. Now that the mother saw the bird hanging too, they set off through the field, walking side by side through the half-grown unbroken weeds the short way there was to go. Ahead stood the trees: it might have been that a fistful of seed, no two alike, had been flung down, years back, upon that place—oak, ash, beech, juniper, elder and their underbrush—and this almost circular island of uneven, incongruous mast and foliage had sprung up there in the open sea of grass. The mother and the girl did not speak as they walked but watched those forward branches of the oak where the bird hung, rising and falling.

"There's a sling on his neck," said the woman, standing under him now and letting the bag drop behind her into the grass.

"They've tried to hang him!" the girl cried out in anger. "Boys, of course! They've strung him up there simply for the fun of it!"

"Rubbish," said the woman. They stood with their heads thrown back, the mother taller, stronger, their faces lifted to the flapping captive bird. "He's got his head tangled in it somehow. He's a thrush—a silly, thieving thrush, out after something for his nest and this is the trouble he's got himself into."

As they stood under him watching, he fluttered wildly upward and lit in panic on the branch above. There he paused, his beak gaping weakly, his eye, bright, wounded, desperate, on them. Below him the string that held him tethered loop down, swinging loose as a hammock on the delicate air.

"So now I suppose you see what you've got yourself into?" the woman called up to him from the ground. "Now you see what it means to go snooping and nosing

around instead of staying in the woods where you belong!"
The bird sat high above them, unmoving on the branch,
his beak as if pried open, his motionless body throbbing
under the leaves like a feathered, stricken heart. "I've a
good mind to leave you right where you are like that,"
she said, and she added: "He's too high to reach from here."

"I can climb to him," the girl said. "I can easily get up
to him."

She leaned and undid her sandals, and then the boy
hands reached up and closed on the oak's lowest bough
and her feet swung off the ground. The bare feet ran
quickly up the trunk's hide and she stood upright in the
first fork with one arm around the tree's girth. Seeing her
there, taller and closer in menace, the bird fell threshing
again from the branch and hung, the eye on her small,
bright, alert, jerking at the string's extremity. It will be
like having a moth fly in the room at night, the girl said
climbing higher; I'll feel the flesh moving up my back and
swear not to shudder and all the time I'll be crawling cold
with terror. When I get my hands around him to lift him
down, I'll have to keep my eyes shut, and even then I
won't be able to bear the feel of his feathers beating and
fluttering on my skin.

"Move out along the branch towards him from where
you are," the mother called up. Her face was lifted and
the sailor-hat brim hung limp across her brow and ears.

"Yes," said the girl, not moving. "That's what I'm going
to do."

Or the feel of his feet, I won't be able to stand it.
They'll be cold, naked, unbearable, like a sick thing's or a
dying baby's fingers. If I touch him I'll have to choke him

in terror, I'll have to break his legs in two, I'll have to do it. She crouched waiting at the tree's second fork before beginning the journey out, her fingers and bare feet holding to the tree's heavy hide. And now, ahead, she could see how the string lay coiled around the branch and the fiber of it, like good fishing-line. Exactly like fishing-gut, she thought, her eyes shifting quickly, steadily from the bird's hanging body beating among the leaves to the way out along the slowly yielding curve of the wood.

"A yard more and you've got him," said the mother, carefully, step by step, keeping pace with her on the ground below; and now the branch sagged gently with the girl's weight, dipped whispering and creaking lower while the mother said cautiously: "Go a little further and then I can reach up and get him."

"But don't pull him!" the girl said. Pausing there, crouched animal-like, wide-eyed on the branch, she saw suddenly what it was. "It is fishing-line!" she said. "Look! He's swallowed the worm and hook, that's what he's done—"

She began unwinding the broken gut string from the bough, squatting on her bare legs and feet and reaching out, and now the terrible, wild, tugging life freed of the branch pulled on the string her hands held, tore through the leaves in frantic terror like a fish leaping underwater with the hook caught in him. In a minute he'll rip his tongue out and I'll go crazy, she thought, feeding the line down to her mother, and below her the woman lifted her arms high and raised her empty hands.

"Can you get him? Have you got him?" the girl said, and she closed her eyes so as to see it no longer and crouched blind, dazed in the tree with the nightmare of frail desperate life tearing, beak, claw, and wing, at the string's vein through her fingers.

"Yes, let the string go," said the mother's hushed voice. "Let it go. I have him," and the movement ceased suddenly, halted with an abruptness closer to extinction than release as the woman took him in her lifted hands.

The girl swung herself from the second branch down to the first, and hung from the first for a moment before dropping to the ground. The woman held him fast, the beak wide open in her fingers while with the right hand she manipulated the hook forked deep within his throat. The breath came audibly through her nostrils as she worked and her face hung over him, and it was at the face the girl looked, not at the bird, as she stood beside her. She looked at the long pale cheek and the lips set and she said, Mother, not speaking aloud, you can touch these things, you can touch death and wipe it off in your handkerchief afterwards and touch pain without shrinking from it but you cannot take me in your arms any more and when I am with you I am afraid. Mother, she said in silence not looking at the bird, come out of your stone flesh and touch me too and see how tall I am, my eye almost up to your eye, and how big my feet and hands are, like a woman's. But the cheek did not alter and did not color, and the girl made herself look down now at the bird. For a while there was no sign of blood, only the stretched gagging throat and tongue, and then suddenly it came, fine as thread and dark across the seemingly unliving substance of the beak and across the cushion of the woman's finger prying it wide.

"There," she said, and she flung the freed hook and the length of the fishing-line from her and lifted the bird closer in her fist to see deeper into the hopelessly defended and betrayed secrets of its throat and sight. And now, eye to eye with her, he closed his beak violently on her finger, the flat tiny poll bristling with outrage, the beak striking and closing and striking again out of the small held feathered body in a paroxysm of hate.

"Now what will he do? Will he be able to eat?" the girl asked in a whisper, watching, and while she said it the woman opened the hand that held him and he struggled queerly forward, his feathers damp from the pressure of the palm and fingers and their human moisture and the thread of black blood streaking across his bill and breast. He did not fly at once: first he soiled the woman's hand and then he wheeled falteringly off under the trees.

"He can't fly straight yet," the mother said, and she stooped and wiped her hand off on the grasses. "Perhaps hanging all night there—"

And now as if the exact hour to speak had struck, as if it were this surprised and perhaps unpermanent moment of tenderness or frailty or default they had been waiting for, the girl put her hand up to the dark hair above her brow, shielding her eyes a little from the absolute committance of sight and began saying:

"Mother, I want to know now, I want to know it so much now so I'll be certain . . . I've been trying to say it to you since I've been back . . . I want to know if you and Candy will let me . . . I want to know it so I can plan about it and talk and write letters . . . I mean, if you will let me go again in September . . . it's June now, I mean in about three months could I . . . I mean, to study somewhere, of course, not just to have a good time but to really learn . . ."

The mother had turned away and stooped, and with her head down picked up the bathing-bag where she had dropped it in the grass.

"Where? Where do you want to go?" she said, her hands dragging the bag's strings tighter, the face turned off under the old hat's brim and the dry lips trembling a little, not speaking loud.

"I thought perhaps back to Florence only not . . . I mean, I don't want to go to Miss Easter's again . . . I thought . . . You see, I want to paint. I thought live with a family in Paris or Florence or somewhere like that and go to classes . . . I thought . . . I mean . . ." She stopped saying it when the mother turned, her chin lifted.

"Nan, don't talk drivel," she said. "Think what you're saying. A girl of your age turned loose in a city. You'd soon enough see the folly of it—"

She was facing the stream again, the path, the willows concealing at the water's bend what lay so richly, ripely, fragrantly beyond. She had begun to move towards it, her back to the girl, the bag swinging, escaping towards the wind's smell, the myriad sound and stamp, the eager substance and heart of horses in their paddocks. Behind her the girl stood waiting, trembling, silent a moment before she too began walking.

"Not loose," she said after her. "Mother, not loose," but the tears rising in her throat stopped the sound of it with pain.

Chapter Two

AFTER she had opened the stable door and let the sun run in she stood watching him an instant: his head was high but quiet, his ears alive, his mahogany flank gleamed richly in the light from the part-opened door. Out of the shallow dimness of the boxes she could hear the groom's voice, continuous in the soothing swageing words of horse-talk as she crossed the floor, hearing it steady as water murmuring while she crossed the separately rounded and hoof-scarred timbers to where the hunter stood beyond his gate. His loins and quarters shone bright and firm and he stood on all four feet, without a hoof cocked, even though at ease. "You Brigand, you troublemaker," she said half-aloud and he turned his head on his shoulder to watch her come inside and close the latch behind her, and then he shifted to one side. At his head she raised her bare arm and laid her hand, gloved to the wrist, beneath his mane.

Now the delusion of darkness was clearing, ebbing fast, as her eyes altered, towards light: she could see the knots in the boards of the stall and the mare's head and neck beyond and her full ripe dappled shoulder over the partitions that stood between, and the strings of white hair, like a witch's, hanging on the brood-mare's neck. "I like this horse, Apby," the girl said, with her hand laid under the hunter's mane. She stood looking beyond into the clearing obscurity at the mare's head and the unseen crouching groom, saying it to his goodafternoon and the voice's low ceaseless cajoling. The windows were open the stable's length and the air was clean with avenues of myriad sparkling light running with sun to the forage of oaten straw and striking there and igniting it like flame. "Apby, I like him. I like the way he went yesterday. He's a good horse," she said. She was wearing breeches, old ones, too tight and darned across the knees, and a sport shirt undone at the neck. The gloves with the buttons missing and the brown leather wearing through white at the fingers' ends were turned inside out at her bare wrists and flapped back loose across her hands.

"Yes, Miss," said the groom, not lifting his voice to say it but letting the sound go murmuring on. "Bees swarming all the morning kept them nervy. They was all over the windows and wood." So hush now, so be still now, it went on gently, gently to the brood-mare as he squatted beside her using the paring-knife on her unshod foot. "Out yonder the wall was black with them, thick," he said in the same low, tempered, wooing tone. "They didn't like them, did you, lady? Oh, not at all, they didn't like them. I got them away with sulphur, burning it here and there in dishes outside and in."

"Apby, what do you think of him as a horse?" the girl said. "What do you think of this animal? He's turned out to be mine." She stood looking into the horse's dark clear eye with the lash, thick, black, fernlike, brushing on the lid, and the blood turned warm, the marrow melted softly in her from the power of the delicate, quick body breathing near. "What do you think of this upstart, this Brigand with his bony face?" she said. The smell of his coat was sweet and the neck's arch sprang firm and meaty underneath her hand.

"I will say he's got a good rein," the groom's voice began saying warily from the brood-mare's side. "He's got quite a bit in front of him, and that gives a horse an air. But I wouldn't—"

"He's got a foolish head, my fine horse has," said the girl with love, and she pulled the near ear gently down and drew the pointed fur tip of it across her face. And now, as if just recognizing the words the groom's voice had shaped or just receiving now their sense on some vague undulation of retarded hearing, she stopped short and stared across the stalls' partitions at the mare's head and shoulder and the unseen groom. "But you wouldn't what?" she said. "You wouldn't what?"

"It might be that I would never have thought of picking him out for a buy," the groom's voice went on. "But if he's stag-faced, as Mrs. Lombe has it, it don't hurt him none for riding. No one's going to ask nothing else of him, the way I understand it." He did not look up, the head, the soiled brown cap lowered over the bent foot as he worked at the mare's side, the same gentle assuaging murmur of contemporation crooning: "If he runs to hollowness towards the nose, there's no foal going to bear it on. Whatever his faults are or his points either, it stops with him there and no harm come to, at least the way I look at it."

She stood with her hand stopped under the black hairs of the mane still, her obsessed rapt gaze moving from the ear's soft flick and the passive brow down the nasal bones to the nostril, her own dream-stupored, half-slumbering eye level with the horse's proud soft brilliant eye. So this is how they think of you, my horse, she said in silence to him. She lifted her other hand and touched the wide hard cheek-bone's blade. Not my first horse or my second or even the third, but this time my horse in protest, my hunter in defiance; not with race and nervousness flickering down your crest and loins, but my bony-legged monster to gentle, to murmur alone to in fortification of my father's errors; the substance of identity and revolt and love to hold to, until I can see you like the oriflamme of what is nothing more violent than Candy and me walking down a street arm in arm together in another country, she said, the gloved hand moving on his neck under the mane's coarse glossy hair. With one finger she lifted the velvet of his lip and looked at the upper teeth laid bare in his mouth, breathing the warm hay-sweetened breath while the physical stab of love thrust in her. He drew his head up from her hand, but tractably, the nostril opening dry as silk and rosy and the hairs quivering on his vulnerable unmottled lip.

"Apby, what age would you give him?" she said, watching in grave passionate pride how his teeth met evenly, touching one on the other almost vertically.

"I'd give him off five," the groom said from the other box, and the girl looked up in sudden sharpness and Brigand's ears flicked on his lifted head.

"Off five!" she said. "What rubbish, Apby! Have you taken the trouble to look at him instead of just making up your mind about him without— Look here, his side front teeth are hardly cut. I'd say he's just off three."

"Come first July I'd give him rising six," the groom said, the peaceful, persistently assuaging voice unaltered. "He's cutting his tush and that's what's maybe thrown you off," but when he heard her jerk the bridle down off the peg he stood up in the mare's box. "I'll have him ready for you straight away, Miss, if you're taking him out," he said.

"No, I'll do it," she said shortly. "I don't see how in the world you handle him at all, feeling about him the way you do." Her hand in its glove lifted the hunter's hair and drew the forelock free of the browband onto his face and buckled the cheek-pieces tighter, working in quick stubborn rebuke. "You'd let them tell you anything and believe it, true or not," she said. She did not look for an instant over the box's panel to where the groom stood, the dwarfed arms hanging from the waistcoat's cramp and the blunt soiled fingers turning the paring-knife in harried, slow humility. He saw the sun coming through the open window onto her hair and head as she loosened the throat-lash on the horse's neck: the dark soft longish hair with the strong light on it and the pale face and throat and the mouth's color warm but pallid and he began saying in expiation:

"They're up to all kinds of tricks you'd never suspect if you wasn't onto them. Copers'll file off the seven-year notch and nobody the wiser if they get hold of a buyer what wouldn't know. You got to keep your eyes open, I tell you, you can't trust anybody, you just got to look sharp." He stood watching her from the other box and turning the paring-knife in his fingers, as if just to keep on talking no matter what the words were would be enough to set it right at last. "Bishoping's another coper's trick," he said. "They'll level the teeth off short and gouge the centers out and blacken them with caustic if they think it'll sell a ten-year old for a six," he said, and then he said abruptly and painfully: "I didn't mean no offense about his age, Miss," standing with the brown cloth cap turned back to front and lending him the look now of a tough stunted gladiator halted in the arena, uncharioted, bewildered, and unarmed. When he said this to her over the box's panel, she raised her lids and looked with the heavy, seemingly drugged wide-spaced eyes across the crib-bitten wood at him, the eyes' substance transparent as glass in the sunlight and clear bright icy blue.

"All right," she said, lifting the saddle over the gate. She stooped to girth it, and now the groom returned to his work again and his voice to cajoling, saying to the mare or the girl or to their quiet This is the way I came to say it or how I came to think it or Here's the explanation of it if you want it and this is the truth, s'help me, soothing them, lulling them, rocking them to sleep with the low half-querulous murmur of his self-palliation as he raised the mare's forefoot onto his lowered knee.

Saddled and bridled the horse waited while she unlatched the gate, and then turned in his box to follow her out. He carried his head down and the reins loose on his neck, but the ears were pointing in expectancy, his hoofs thudding loud and full on the timber as he came. His sloping shoulders flowed under the loose burnished skin and on the left side of his neck his mane hung dark and glossy. At the stable door the girl turned and took the double reins and ran them over her arm; when she lifted the door's handle and pushed the half of it out, the daylight fell like a wedge through the stable's dark.

"Apby," she said, looking back, and the groom stood up and answered, "Yes, Miss," touching his cap as he stood helpless, hopeless in the box by the mare. "Brigand's my show now," she said. "I'll be in to do him every morning," and the groom answered bleakly, "Yes, Miss" again, and touched his cap again with his fingers, and then he suddenly began saying: "Sometimes even old hands at the game'll make a slip, like a breeder I knew of once was thrown off by the corner teeth. You'll see them coming through around four years and rising five, nine times out of ten you will, but like this time I was speaking about, there was the exception proving the rule, as they say, and knowing the horse I knew when he was foaled, a bay colt nice as anything you've seen—"

"All right," the girl said from the doorway, the voice cold, implacable still.

"That Brigand there, he has the kind of look like he might break a rule," the groom said, speaking louder as if the mere sound of his impetration must set it right no matter what the words were. "When Mr. Lombe brought him in a month or something back, I said right off to Mrs. Lombe, I said if ever I saw a horse that looked like he'd—"

"All right," she said, stepping clear of the beam. "All right." She watched the horse pick his way over after her and she said: "All right, Apby, I'll see to him myself when I bring him in. Don't wait around for him," and she closed the door.

✦

Candy Lombe had put his dark green felt on looking at himself, the roundish, soft, bright face, the swollen aggrieved eyes, looking straight into the vestibule's long glass and bringing the brim down right; the small hand with

the signet dark red ring drawing tighter the cravat on which
the beagles ran against his throat, the head held back to
get the light while he slipped his fingers along the short
mustaches' bristles on his upper lip and smelled the bay
rum and the shaving-soap that lingered. He had gone off
from the house in the afternoon feeling the curse lying
heavy on him: the bane and the wrong that there was no
shape to his life and none in the past since youth (and
youth shaped by what, after all, but the imminence of
hope), and now youth gone and the curse of nothing else
to come. The forty-three or forty-four years (he couldn't
or didn't want to remember which) must for a long time
now have been these fragments, discarded over some vague
period of space or time: vestiges of a thing as irreplacable
as life that had been given him entire and that he had let
fall, the separate pieces lost in separate countries, before
knowing there was any value to the thing or even that he
carried anything at all.

Ah, trouble, trouble, there are the two different kinds
of it, he thought, going bitterly alone up through the green
June fields; there's the one you give and the other you
take. I gave, I gave freely, he said to the curse, the bane,
the wrong of his life. It is more blessèd to give than to
receive, so I gave. I gave trouble at home until I was twenty
for the ordeal of art alone; not for the fact or the accomplishment of art but the organized slaughter of what the
idle said was not Art, the Glorified, the Exalted; I gave
trouble year after year for the willful murder of what They
(family) recognized as comfort like a mouse its hole by
Me (individual) who must (for what reason time has never
made clear) be saved from mediocrity for the crowning

and the final wide and loud acclaim. I wore a smock and a beret on the streets of Montreal, did Candy Lombe, by God, and what is he now but a squire in his English squire's jacket strolling up the country with a good felt hat on telling himself he'll get a thumb-nail sketch, a bird's eye view instead of a kick in the seat for his forty-odd years of caring, not making the pretense any more of carrying a water-color box or a palette and tubes and boards but out with his golf hose fitting his ankles right and his heart gone rotten in him.

Because nobody ever made me understand that it was up to me and nobody ever helped me with it or told me what to do, said the petulance, the querulousness which even rising anger could not dignify with heat; me, colonial in England, pauper, painter, each imposing their segregation from country, status, convention. Everyone with their hands lifted hard and high against what I have to be: the intruder on somebody else's soil when I should have stayed home and gone on with what my father was (the visionary, the preacher), and the intruder on some woman's money even if I did give her my name in exchange, and the last tentative intrusion made and abandoned on some other kind of man's career. Me, the painter, tradition of Goya, Velasquez, me, charcoal sketching in night-schools, water-painting landscapes up to thirty like a school-boy, hanging up little canvases in fancy rooms with decorated peasant china and hand-embroidered table linen, all for sale, even the pretty pastel-colored canvases, all at a price for the ladies who come in to tea. Me, an artist, never able to memorize right the lines I wasn't intended to speak or recognizing the cues when I heard them, but somehow trying to take part in the performance, making my exits and entrances blushing, stammering, always backwards and on the wrong side of the stage.

The lane he had come into now had wild hedge growing thick on either side of it and ruts cutting deep and dry into its bed. Long pale grasses sprang up in the crescents marked by draught-horses' feet on the center rise of ground between the stone-hard troughs their cart wheels had hollowed. In a while he knew he would come out onto the dairy farm, not suddenly but piece by piece upon it: first the wall with the moss along it beginning to wind in low, unbroken meandering beyond the orchard trunks, the stones washed light as lime but slightly golden, and after the flash of a white cat with a striped auburn tail past the milk-tins tilted up to sweeten in the sun; step by step coming to it, the familiarly rain-drenched or else the shimmering completely silent, rural scene. It might have been something printed on a postcard, or still more a faintly tinted photograph joined by a silk cord with tassels to a wall calendar for the year. C. Lombe, Esq., he said walking measuredly in silence towards it, taking his forty-three or forty-four years of protest against, dreams of, demands for whispered or spoken or cried aloud at night, to this stage laid for still unaccumulated action, to this hushed homely amphitheater where the classic drama of neurosis might play itself out to destruction; Candy Lombe taking the not even colossal failure of these expended years out for a stroll this afternoon as I did yesterday afternoon and as I will take it out into the air tomorrow, exactly as you'd take a horse out, two hours of gentle exercise a day, to tire him for his body's peace and wear him down to time's passivity for his soul's. Lure the days one after another like this, as the years have been inveigled to a lonely spot where their cries cannot be heard and cut their throats for them and fling them, virgin still, upon the manure-heaps, the stable-rakings, the horse offal of this part of England. They can't stink more than stud-farms do of sex and monstrous matings and foalings brutaler than murders.

Through his shoes he could feel the scars the horses' irons had left in the lane-bed's clay, the shape of them set hard into his shoe leather like in his memory: the calkins, the feather-edge, the plain, the Rodway shoe. Nowhere in this countryside could you get away from the mark of horses on the soil, the smell of horses, of horses' droppings, the rose-headed and counter-sunk shoe-nails found on the roads and lanes and scattered through the pastures. Horses pulled carts when I was young, he thought, walking; they were nothing to me, neither to be liked or not. They never entered into life's substance; their place was allotted, not mine. They were not the established order and I the outcast lost to society and human intercourse for want of a proper name. And now, to elude their wild extravagant possession, Candy Lombe instead of signing canvases walks through a county fetid with horse, rank with horse, pockmarked and stampeded by them; here he is, paddocked at middle-age, hobbled without a choice of pasture or forage, buckled and strapped and gelded and going thick in the wind.

"I feel so sorry for Candy, although he looks such a dandy," he began, making it up, half aloud. "His squire's jacket is black and white, and his something something fits him tight—right—I feel so sorry for Candy," he started over again, "although his color's so—though his color's fresh and dandy. His hair and his mustache are neat, but he's sick of the sight of horses' feet. I feel so VERY sorry for him—tum-te-tum, te-tum-te-tum. He used to be young and his paunch was thin, but rigs and fillys have done him in. I feel so sorry for—"

Now the first sight of the dairy began through the apple trees and he stopped making his verses up and watched for the wings and the dreamy faintly blowing back-drop and the familiar properties set to the right and left. There was the stage, the rural lovely scene, and no players on the boards yet, as yet no sign of horse-dirt fouling the prepared ground here where the lane widened slowly towards the farm's court and halted. Oh, Candy Lombe, he used to paint, he said to himself, the idle English gentleman wandering towards the picturesque little dairy farm on the June afternoon. But all the praise he got was faint. He thought: if I stop saying this I'm lost, if I stop saying Oh, Candy Lombe, he used to think in the days before he took to—if I stop saying it I'll see the curse hanging there before me, weighted and choked with death and incongruous in the sun as a corpse hanging in his old clothes behind the house there by his neck and swinging gently, or a railway tramp lying iron-dead in a freight-car of red apples. Oh, Nancy, Nancy, give me ear, he went on, like whistling in the dark; oh, hasten to your father, dear! Oh, Candy Lombe stepped out from home, he began rapidly again, and then he saw the first movement of life, furtive and quick as something stirring in the twilight of early morning or evening: the white cat flashing past the up-turned milk-tins as it had done yesterday afternoon, only a little earlier, just as he had been a few yards back crossing the orchard grass. Now, it seemed, had the overture to action been executed at last, and immediately the ducks, neat and immaculate as linen, reeled slowly around the corner of the dairy farm-house and started for the water-trough.

After a time, still standing there in his gray knickerbockers and his trimly gartered wool hose and watching the ducks beguile themselves gravely across the water's surface, their bills dipping and fumbling below the brink, he began to hear the sound of the horse's hoofs coming. For a while he did not turn his head to see or even begin conjecturing, but stood with his hands in his jacket pockets, the narrow, cleanly manicured thumbs showing, the hat-brim smartly down, seeming to watch the ducks in the water but perhaps seeing nothing beyond the lost, corrupted vision of his youth or hearing nothing but the sound of its despair. But when the horse had come close behind him and the rider drew rein, he started and turned in guilt, his right arm involuntarily raised partly in some gesture of greeting and partly as if to ward off the violence of actual sight or being seen by whomever had come on him undefended and unaware.

"Hello, Candy," said Nan from the horse's back, and here were their eyes meeting down the slant of the mahogany shoulder, the same marvelously glazed, indolently cast eyes obliquely and rather shyly spanning the distance's acclivity from mount to ground, and their mouths smiling.

"Why, hello there, Nancy," the father said with an American and disproportionate heartiness that only from uneasiness and hesitation sought to cloak, conceal, secrete nothing but the soul's timidity.

"I was looking for you," the girl said. "I rode him up here because I thought you came this way."

"I've got the habit of walking up here in the afternoons," he said in a bright sociable tone, almost but not quite as if seeking to keep from her some reason for his having come. He laid one hand, palm down, on the horse's shoulder and looked up at her from under the smartly dipping fine felt brim. "Gets me away from the stud," he said, his small mouth and his chin beginning to laugh under his mustache. "I think it's more like country up here and not so much like business. Nobody's doing anything, not even the ducks." He was smiling up at her with this little defense, this eager little reserve between them as if she were a lady he had just met at tea. "I can flâner les boulevards, as it were," he said. When he put out his hand to hold the rein while she dismounted, she stopped and said:

"Don't hold him. Please, don't hold him. He won't stir."

"You've only ridden him two days," said Candy, but he stayed his hand uncertainly and watched her slide to the ground.

"He's been very nicely trained, your horse has," she said. "When I mount he stands without moving a muscle while I fix my reins or gloves or belt or fiddle with the stirrups." She brought the reins forward over the horse's head and ran them up her arm. "We did exercises at the trot this afternoon: the figure of eight on one track and hock turns and the turn about. We're getting on very well together." They walked along side by side, past the dairy farmhouse, the girl with the horse coming docilely behind her and the man with his hands in his jacket pockets, side by side out onto the country road. "Only voices worry him a little. He

likes them soft and low, like you do." Their eyes slid sideways again at each other's faces, and the father laughed.
"He shied twice—once at a fence and at a tree back there a
minute before the dairy. I told him I wouldn't have it."

"Now, listen," said Candy. "I don't want him to get you
into trouble." Here it was, the threat, the menace of horses
again, the monstrous promise in their bone and hide of the
mutilation, the even fatal evil they could wreak on peace
sounding alarm from nerve to nerve and marking it in trepi-
dation on his face. "Look here, Nancy, I want you to be
careful with him."

"It's just a game he likes to play," she said. "He pretended
he couldn't get the look of the fence right and so he shied
off at the jump. He must have seen other horses' dem-
onstrations, you know, and thinks it's smart to imitate them
—you know, the way schoolgirls, I mean some do, you
know, the way they imitate or pretend to talk like picture
actresses they've seen—"

"The silly, adolescent creatures," Candy said severely.

"Ah, don't laugh," his daughter said, and the horse came
gently, meekly on behind. "He's looking for a personality,
you know, the way you have to when you're young. You
can't always decide so quickly what you're going to be like.
Sometimes he plays at being willful and he goes on the way
he must have seen race horses do. But it doesn't mean anything, it's really rather silly of him. Coming up the hill he
stopped walking and stared at a clump of buttercups as if
he'd never seen anything like them before, or perhaps as if
he couldn't *really* see them, and then he just walked on and
I couldn't get a word out of him. But he's really, I mean
underneath everything else, he's really awfully afraid of dis-

pleasing. You can see by looking at him he's very vain," she said.

"Oh, can you?" said Candy, looking back under the brim of his hat at the horse coming on behind. "Now, with all due respect, Nancy, where—"

"Ah, don't make fun of him!" she said in sudden pain. "Everyone ridiculing him and jeering at him as if he were the stable freak simply because he isn't to sire or foal or isn't a colt, or isn't to train, or hasn't a single action he's expected to perform! Simply to look the fool and hack around, but I didn't think you'd feel that about him—"

Walking in silence beside her, he put his arm in the black-and-white patterned sleeve through her bare arm's bend and drew her against him until he felt the ribs and the breast under the sport shirt moving against his squire's cloth, walking in step with her and in silence, the sharp small daughterly hip moving against his thickening hip.

"Nancy, I'm sorry. I'm sorry I said that," he said. "I didn't mean it." A freak and a fool and a hack like me, he thought in bitter, retributive guilt. In this way they walked on for a while through the scallops of shade and sun, shade cast by the thickly arching trees and sun shining palely in the open spaces on the ground; each thinking of the horse, not as it came along behind them at the end of its loose rein, but transformed to symbol for the separateness of two interpretations and two isolate despairs. "I was thinking this afternoon," the father said, "about horses. You were brought up on the brutes but I wasn't. I never had a horse anywhere near me, except pulling a milk-wagon or a tramcar, when I was young. Perhaps I keep on thinking about horses without knowing that I think of them like that, the way someone who has all the equipment bought and ready and has promised to go big-game hunting feels when he starts thinking about the game, you know, the elephants and the lions and all that. Of course, I mean somebody who doesn't like big-game hunting or big game or who doesn't even like shooting. I mean, somebody who just simply doesn't like to think about lions and elephants and other big savage animals and who would rather think about something else. Well, there it is," he said, beginning to smile uneasily under his mustache. "So I have to get out of it by being funny about horses. If I wasn't funny about them I'd have to get up and ride one and I never liked getting anywhere near them. I've climbed up on them for almost twenty years, and I respect them, they stand very high in my opinion, and I think they've got all the qualities the horse authorities claim they have. But I just don't like having much to do with them. I like to watch a good point-to-point race or a steeplechase and have some money on it, but I don't like getting into mix-ups with them. Maybe it's because I'm not really interested in showing them, you know, or anybody I'm the master. I don't like to bully anything into obeying me so that's why I don't like to have to go into their stalls or have too much to do with them. I don't mind this chap coming along behind us here because he's not as arrogant as most, but I wouldn't go out of my way—"

"I met a man last winter," the girl said, his arm through hers as she walked, her eyes watching the ground. "He'd been brought up with them, like me." They went on, arm in arm, silent for a little further and the horse came following on his rein. "At Mrs. Paddington's Wednesday teas in Florence, I met him there," she said after a minute. "He was an Irishman—about twenty or something like that. His people kept hunters and his mother had one of the best seats in Ireland, she was one of the grand women to hounds—you know, he didn't say it to brag but like a joke," she said, looking quickly at the side of her father's face. "As a matter of fact, he couldn't stick hunting. It made him sick. And I knew I felt that way too, after he'd said it, only I'd never been able to explain it before. He'd gone off from home after a row, I think, or something, but anyway he couldn't stick the kind of hunting county people he'd been born with. He was writing a book about them. He was one of the first writers I ever met," she said.

Arm in arm, step by step they went on together, and the father's eyes slipping sideways saw the tender flesh of her neck, and the ear's lobe pale as coral, and the vulnerable temple with life beating visibly, exquisitely there. He made his tone carefully, casually bright so as not to scare her words off.

"Sounds like an interesting sort of chap," he said, clearing his throat and watching the ground below.

"Candy," said the girl in a quick, soft, eager voice, but she did not turn her head. "I want to go back in September. I don't mean back to Miss Easter's but back to Paris or somewhere else. I want to do something. I have to do something. I can't stay here. I mean, I want to go on studying painting or art or maybe how to be a sculptor and I thought after a while I might be able to make my living and then I wouldn't have to stay all the year here. It's not," she said, not looking up from the road but watching it go steadily beneath their walking feet, "I mean, it hasn't anything to do with not—with not loving you or not loving anyone, but in cities and

41

in other places, you know, there're people all over the world, I mean like that Irishman, saying different things all the time and here nobody hears them saying them and—"

"Nancy," said the father in a tight, small, but brightly casual voice. "I suppose—that is, if it's true I thought you just might like to say it—I suppose it's possible you liked him rather well?"

"Oh, no," she said quickly. "I didn't mean that. I only saw him two or three times after that. He wasn't staying long in Florence. He was on his way to Spain." Arm in arm they walked, watching the ground move back beneath their feet, the road slipping back and away in the shade and the light and the shade from the trees as they walked small and human-voiced and human-limbed under the high fresh springing boughs. "He was going to get over there and fight against Franco, only he couldn't let the Italians hear him say it. Here you wouldn't know about anybody doing anything like that, would you, Candy? Or if you read it in the paper you'd forget about it because you wouldn't have the sound of the person's voice when they said it or how their face looked."

"No," said Candy, holding her arm tight in his. "No. I know."

"So I thought if I could do something, do some kind of work, I mean first learn to do something, like painting, the way you did," she went on, watching the ground go; and Like me, he thought, learn to sit waiting in a room alone, face a blank canvas and a notebook with a sketch or two sketches in it, the brushes clean, the paints ready, the light right, the easel set, and sit there making no mark, and fearing to make any, and sit fearing thought as impotently as act. Learn to sit still in terror before nothing, learning, the way a convict learns by heart the words of his sentence, the emptiness of one's own indecision and the elusiveness of the idiom, the pronunciation, the sound even of one's own purposeless intention. "So I thought if I could go back over there, I mean to Paris or Rome or somewhere in September," she was saying, and he went on in silence: Learn it without ever crying out in protest or bringing down in vengeance, and slowly, weakly, gradually meander to the first drink of consolation and the second, until Drink itself becomes the thing to wait for in the room's and soul's void, not the visitation youth promised of the pure and perfect substance of Art. "I thought if it could be decided now so that I'd know," she was saying, "then I could stick it out here this summer without—"

The road moved slowly, unevenly off behind them through light and shade, shade and shimmering afternoon light, poured slowly back over rut and scarcely covered stone as they walked with their heads down, the same shapely, well-turned flesh and bone, the same drugged dreamy eyes watching it run slowly, endlessly back beneath their feet.

"Yes, that's the way I must have felt," said the father. "Just about your age—almost thirty years ago, maybe about twenty-seven or -eight years back—"

"I could get a room with a family or something or live in a club," the girl said. "Then you wouldn't worry about that part of what was happening to me. You could come over with me, Candy, and find the right courses for me to take, and meet the teachers and find the place for me to live in." She was talking faster now, her breath coming quick, as if the name of the street, the size of the room, the utensils of the art itself would be designated in a minute if she could catch up with where they were. "Candy, you could even find out for me what it is I ought to do," she said, and her mouth trembled.

"Yes," said her father, holding her bare arm tight in the up-bend of his arm, his fingers lying on her wrist. "You'll have to find somebody very good; you mustn't have somebody vague to teach you the things you'll have to learn. You know, bone's there, structure's there," he said brightly, his fingers modeling at her wrist where the pulse beat light and quick in the veins. "The old skeleton's there under the rest; under all the fanciness and vagueness you've got to find out in the end that he's there and how he goes together and how he moves. That's what I never paid enough attention to, Nancy. Perhaps that's why I never made a go of things." He glanced quickly, uneasily at the side of her face, and then away, thinking Perhaps it's too late already, perhaps there is nothing more to conceal from her by now. Ever since she could think for herself, maybe, she's laid in her bed at night knowing what I am better than I've ever known it, seeing me clearer, thinking about the one water-color hanging up in the top-hall and the one in the guest room behind the door, and knowing exactly without anyone saying it to her. Out loud he said in bold shy uneasiness: "You've got to dig right down into things from the start if you want to get anywhere. I tried out too many things, got interested in one phase of a thing—you know, experimented with one thing after another, and sometimes that leads you nowhere. I might have done a lot of things if I'd got hold

44

of something certain at the outset. I might have done some
good paintings—"

"Candy, you are a great painter," the girl said gravely.

"Oh, no," he said, looking down at the road and the little
twitching smile beginning on his lips. "Oh, no."

For a time they had forgotten the horse, hearing without
knowing they heard the slow light clopping of his hoofs
behind them, but now the rein tightened on her arm and
she stopped and looked back to where the horse stood
halted on the road. His head was raised and turned a little
to one side, away, and when she said his name he shook it
gently, then savagely, in bewilderment. He stood fixed at
his rein's length, like a beast who has come to water and
will not cross, the forefeet planted in advance of the full
glossy breast, the shocked hoofs gripping forward for balance to the earth. He had not started to retreat yet and did
not venture to come on, but stood, his legs thrusting wider
and wider apart, the neck curved back burnished, voluptu-
ous as a swan's, and the raised head tossing, gently, gently,
as if seeking to cast the mask of unfamiliar and desperate
confusion off.

"Brigand," said the girl softly, drawing in the rein. "Brig-
and, you foolish thing, be quiet now, be still."

She had turned to him and now began walking to him,
but once the rein had slackened on his mouth he reeled
slowly, sickeningly backwards on his heels, the last link with
human ascendancy and human corporality withdrawn, leaving him staggering masterless, lost, riderless in the obscure
and incommunicable reaches of his pain.

"Look out for him!" the father suddenly cried out. "Get
away from him, Nancy!" She saw him make the jump for-

ward, the color ebbed from his face and mouth, and jerk the rein from her hand, and saw the horse whirl in panic and totter towards the ditch and trees and falter, as if sensing not seeing danger there, and stop quivering on the brink. "Get away from behind him! He may start kicking, Nancy!" Candy called out. "He's had a stroke! Look out for him! He's going to fall!"

"Hush," she said savagely. "Hush, oh, hush," to man and beast and to the terror that palsied their bones. She was at the horse's head again, taking the man's clutched trembling fingers from the leather and drawing the rein's length from his hand. "Hush, now stop, now listen to me," she said, and at the sound of her voice the horse's head veered awkwardly, but meek, despairing, towards her, the ears quivering antennae-vulnerable, the raised face defeated, directionless, blind, mute. "Hush now," she said, "hush now," standing bare-armed, bare-headed between the man's and the horse's terror of each other and the terror of what mystery, violent, powerful, unstayed, had struck like paralysis with a hand numb as stone and might lift again and strike before them. "Hush now," she said, and she brought the horse's head slowly down and, talking, slipped her gloved fingers under the browband and the fore-lock's length of straight black hair. The gloved leather came away wet, darkened as if from the touch of blood, and the girl stood looking at it. "Sweat," she said, half-aloud, staring at her hand. "He hasn't been running and still sweating like that. . . ."

"Nancy," said the father, running his tongue along his lip. "Nancy, for God's sake, let him go."

"He's got himself into a fever, so he has, my lamb, my lamb," she said, holding his soft mouth and his head firm

46

in the reins caught underneath his chin. "He's been worrying and worrying himself about worms or thinking about his family tree," she said, stroking the bony, prow-like nasal peak, thinking *In a moment Candy may start shouting again or the thing that has struck once strike harder like a crop splitting skull and fiber across the frontal bone.* "He's been eating too much, my horse has, and given himself the mad and sleepy staggers, so he has. He's got himself into a fit and he'd like a drink of water, that's what he'd like," she went on saying, thinking *I must go on talking so that there's no time for anything else and no place for any other sound, I must go on in this voice because this is the voice that says to him,* "So now we'll just go quietly along home because nothing has happened to my big foolish man, we'll just give him some salt and a bucket of warm water to soothe him and we'll rub his belly for him and rub him down with a straw wisp—"

"Nancy," said the father, saying it quietly now, not in a voice from which fear had gone but into which more awe than fear had come. "Look at him closely, Nancy," he said, half whispering it. He was fumbling in his pocket for something and the girl looked away from him, wondering, and up at the horse's head again. Holding him under the quivering soft lip, she looked at the bony brow with the moist forelock on it and the searching, flicking ears; looked at the hollows, throbbing and pit-like, above the eyes, and lingered on the fixed brown brilliant eyes themselves before descending the face's sharp decline to the concave nostrils, dilated, convulsed now with pain. "Look at his eyes, Nancy," Candy said, having found the matchbox and holding it in his hand, his fingers shaking still as he drew the frail match-stem along the box's side and cupped the flame against the air's movement underneath the trees. When he lifted his arm the horse gave no sign, but as the match rose higher in her father's hand, the girl began talking again in precaution, murmuring to him in the ceaseless, gentle, assuaging voice that said:

"So his mother must just take him back to his stable and cool him off and put straw under his rug for him and rub him clean and dry and give him . . ."

"Watch him," said Candy softly, and now the match's flame, made puny by the sun's light through the leaves but steadily burning, came level with the horse's eye and halted and he made no sign. "He can't see it," the father said, awe-stricken, scarcely breathing. "He doesn't even know it's there."

Chapter Three

I KNOW we had quite a time of it," the mother was saying, sitting with her knees spread wide so that the rain would dry from her tweed skirt; talking to them while she smoked the cigarette, but half-musingly, only part given to this communication with other beings and part to her own high scrupulous contriving as she looked into the fire on the hearth. "We had one surprise after another from the moment we set foot on shore. In the first place, nobody'd given us any idea we were going to be sewed up in our clothes—"

"Ha, ha," sounded the vet's uneasy laughter, and perhaps because he caught sight of his boots below him on the rug thick with stable and road muck although he had cleaned them off on the mat outside the door, he shifted in cramped, miserable unease on the edge of the ancient shabbily upholstered chair. "Well, I should think that would have been a bit of a shock," he said, and the pale light-lashed eyes sought rather desperately for comfort around the room.

"I must say, I shan't forget it as long as I live," said Mrs. Lombe. She looked up from her contemplation of this other, this unspoken thing, and went on talking lightly of their trip, some or all of which the vet must have heard at other times, in box or paddock, or seated like this in this room. "They packed our feet and legs up in straw the very first thing," she said, "and then this garment arrangement we each of us had to put on was pulled up over the three layers of wool around our bodies and arms—" She went on making the gestures, the mouth open in speech, the words coming quickly, almost merrily; only when she looked up at her husband's and her daughter's faces did it whet to irritation in the strained, impatient eyes. This is the way to meet it, the limbs at ease in the wool skirt and the casual, ordinary cigarette and the conversational manner might have been saying: if you have to face the truth for once in your lives, accept it like this with the chin up and all flags flying from the mast; don't sit there making a tragedy of it. But the eyes ringed deep with a yearning implacable as intolerance knew and had for a long time bitterly and irritably known the uselessness of asking this or anything in reason of them. There they sat on the sofa, a little back, father and daughter facing across the rug's and the table's interval straight at the fire without seeming to see it or seeming to hear what was said. "And then they sewed us right up inside of all this," she went on saying to the vet, the blond raw-skinned young man who sat with his arms placed on his knees and his head extended over his big-wristed, uneasily clasped hands. "Stitched us up for three weeks," she said with a snort of amusement at their own audacity. "Three weeks of it! I tell you, it was an experience to have had."

"Good heavens, three weeks!" the vet echoed in a voice gone high and unbecoming in this attempt at social grace. He glanced in hope towards Mr. and Miss Lombe to see if they were joining in at last, but having seen their faces again he quickly looked away. He drew one hand slowly over the light stubble on his clefted buckling chin and swallowed, thinking now as he had been thinking without interruption that it wasn't to hear stories about where the family had been one spring that he'd come, but to see the hunter and that he'd seen it and he'd told them and the act to be performed was still there undone. But here they sat with the rain falling down outside, talking of Finland or sitting in silence, and coming no nearer to it.

"Of course, we'd taken all sorts of jackets and warm things up there but we were told to leave them where they were. They told us there wasn't any sense in us taking them out of our boxes, but just to leave them there at the hotel the way they were until we got back." She repeated the word "hotel" in sudden derision, jerking her head up from the fire again and giving the lot of them the same queer, anxious, admonishing look. "Hotel, if you please," she said. "It was a lamentable place, as you can imagine, and even for that part of the world it was just about as bad as anything could be. But that's what they called it, for the sake of appearances, I suppose, and that's where we left all our belongings, and I must say I wondered. Mr. Lombe and I had quite a laugh over it," she said and she dropped her cigarette into the fire and struck the ashes from her skirt. "We had no idea if we'd ever see any of our things again, but apparently that was the way it had to be done. Fortunately for us, there were some other English people in the party and they said they'd heard from friends who'd been out to Finland that it was always done like that. And then in the morning there was another shock in store for me," she went on. "They produced the reindeer and I really had no idea, judging from pictures and photographs where one pays more or less attention, you know, I simply hadn't imagined for a moment that a reindeer would be just about the size of a good-sized dane. I'd always thought of them as quite imposing-looking animals, something rather in the cattle line, of course, not so big as a horse," she said, and then she stopped, leaving the word suddenly there, unexpectedly bleak and alone. For an instant she could not look at any one of them but reached out for the poker's handle and took it and thrust it toward the steadily burning wood. Sitting with her knees spread in her skirt and her face turned from them, she struck the log smartly apart and the vet at least saw from his chair the sparks shower across the deep dead ash in the hearth and the chips of charred wood fall forward, smoking, on the stone. Now at the far end of the room the wind and rain drove hard against the windows, and refusing to think That horse, that crazy hunter is standing out there in the stable, stone-blind, incurable, bat-blind, Mrs. Lombe took up from where it had lapsed her own strained, almost merry locution of the other story. "Then they told us, once we'd got over that shock, that we were to lie flat down on the sleds, each one on his own individual sled, you understand, right behind the reindeer's heels." She hung the poker upright in its place again and with the side of one brogue pushed a charred bit of wood back where it belonged. "We each of us had our own separate sleds and reindeers, you see, and when they got us stretched out like that, more like Egyptian mummies than humans by that time as a matter of fact, they started to tuck us in! I kept looking at Mr. Lombe and wondering how he was going to like it!" Having achieved a certain jocularity again, she could look up at the vet and look at Candy Lombe (perhaps at him because in his fear of the heels and hoofs and the power of beasts she had one on him), but not quite yet at the girl's grave, pale, set face. "I told him I'd heard in Russia you landed the other way 'round, that is with your head to the front, guiding the thing with some kind of contraption with your hands, and your face practically under the reindeer's back heels, but that didn't seem to reassure Mr. Lombe, and I must say there were moments when I wondered how it was all going to turn out. As long as we trotted along on the flat it was clear enough sailing, but when we'd start off down those slopes at the pace they kept up, the sleds would begin going faster than the reindeer did, and that had its drawbacks! But the reindeer were beautifully trained and I must say they managed very cleverly. As soon as they felt you outstripping them from behind, they'd jump to one side of the track, skip into the snow at the side to keep you from running right under their heels. It was quite a lark, I thought," she said. "We were four days and nights on the way, sleeping right out in the snow, and we were told that some years at the roundup the wild deer stampeded. They assured us that nobody, that is, no foreigners had ever come to any harm, but the more I thought about it during that drive, the more relieved I was I hadn't taken my daughter with me." And now, having spoken the word daughter, having avowed in some distorted mimicry of declaration I care, I care! she could raise her head and look over the piece of rug and across the gate-legged table on which the Dresden dancers, the woman in a milk-white petticoat, several layers of china thick and edged with lace, on which hung flowered paniers, and the man in blue silk tails danced in formal motionless precision; looked past the vet's clasped raw uneasy hands, his arms and elbows planted on his breeches' knees, his lowered pale-haired head, to where the girl sat in her dark skirt and jersey on the sofa. There the mother's halted look pressed urgently, compellingly, and finally faded to grievousness on her. "She was about fourteen then, and those nights out in the cold, quite an experience for her of course but not quite, you know, just a bit on the rigorous side for a growing and not very robust girl. In fact, I'm not so sure any of the women liked it as much as they said they did. I loved it, but there were two Frenchwomen among us and I'm sure they must have found it very different from what they were accustomed to, their hairdressing shops and café life and everything like that."

The two others, the father and daughter, sat on the sofa motionless still; still sitting a little apart from each other, seeming to hear nothing, see nothing, like people waiting in a hospital's or prison's halls without hope but in numb un-recalcitrant endurance for the verdict to be given. When I got him into the stable last evening, the girl was repeating to herself, saying it slowly and carefully over and over as if this precision had been exacted by a judge and jury or by the gravity of life or death, I thought I must start right off doing everything for him exactly the way it's always been done so he won't think the thing that's happened to him is going to make him any different. I thought, even if he's lost the power so see, and now the word constricted like a knot jerked tighter in her: blind, gone blind, stone-blind. (Stick to the story, please, said the cold hard silent core of listening in rebuke. Tell us what actually took place, don't tell us what you thought.) I got him into his box, she went on looking straight before her across the room, and I began grooming him right away. I didn't want him to suspect yet

54

there was anything the matter, I mean, I thought if I led him home like that, talking to him, and not riding him, he'd see it wasn't the world and the world's paraphernalia that had been wiped out or had been altered even but something as temporary and personal as a toothache that had occurred. (Very well, said the Court, bringing its mallet impatiently down. Get on with it without any dramatization, please.) I started to brush and comb him hard, the girl went on, and then when I saw the brush was annoying him because the prickles were worn down, I asked Apby for another and he handed me a new one over the gate. Apby was standing there watching me all the time I was doing Brigand down, and I did it thoroughly, it took me an hour to do it. There's a sign hanging up in the stable, my mother had it printed and put up there, and it says, "No one can groom a horse without perspiring over it," and by half an hour I was hot and I stopped and took my handkerchief out and wiped my face dry. I knew when you come into the stable in the morning after the grooming's been done you pass your hand through the coat the reverse way to see if it's been properly done, and if you see the gray line there near the hairs' roots you make the groom start his work over again, and I know Brigand was as clean as anything when I was through. After that I thought I'd never let anyone else ever, as long as I was alive and he was alive, I'd never let anyone put a hand on him again. (Please keep to the facts, said the judge or the jury's silence in jobation to her. The Court cannot admit as evidence the passage of thought, however sentimental its trend, through your mind or that of any witness.) So then I told Apby to bring me the warm water, she said, looking straight ahead. I knew I had to sponge Brigand's eyes out because if I avoided doing that, that would be the worst thing. Maybe he'd just been waiting to see if I would do it and if I would touch his eyes, and so I did it and while I did it I spoke to him in a natural tone of voice and I could see the film that was coming over his eyes now, a sort of milkiness blurring them all over, but I went right on sponging out his nostrils and then I did his dock and washed his feet. While I was drying the heel of one forefoot, he reeled a little as if he had lost his balance and he trod back on me, catching my shoe underneath his hoof. I didn't make a sound, I swear I didn't, because I thought it would be the end of him if he thought that having lost the power to see had done this other thing to him too, I mean, had crippled and disabled his legs under him or taken his sense of gravitation from him. I didn't want him to—(Unless you are willing to testify in the manner which the Court has specified, said the controlled cold accents of authority, the evidence you have given will be struck from the records as irrelevant.) Then I brushed the mane and tail, the girl repeated slowly and carefully, and took the burrs out, separating as nearly as I could each hair in his mane and bidding him keep his head low which he did. After laying the mane with water, I brushed the tail out lock by lock from the roots, talking to him about it. I decided to wash his tail at the seven o'clock grooming in the morning, that is this morning, and pick his feet out outside the stable in the sun. But this morning it began raining early, so I did not do this. Last evening then, about half-past six it was, I put his feed down myself for him. I gave him three pounds of corn and a bit over a pound of chop, and because of what had happened to him I gave him a linseed mash. I put his food on the ground for him, just the way he always had it. Apby said it would be better maybe to put his rations up in a manger or hayrack where he could find them easier, and he said he'd bring the portable rack in, but I wouldn't have it. Our horses have always eaten from the ground the way they would if they were turned out to grass and I said I was going to feed him from the ground so he'd go on thinking it couldn't be as bad as he'd thought at first or else everything wouldn't be going on exactly the same. My father had put the call in to Pellton for the veterinary-surgeon to come and I waited in the stable to see if Brigand was going to eat, and he snuffed around for a bit and after I'd talked to him he put his head down to where the food was because he knew it had always been there although now he was blind, do you understand, he was stone-blind, he couldn't see it— (Very well, said the unmoved, the untouched silence, that will be all, Miss Lombe, that will do.) But I have to tell you this! the girl cried out, and she jumped up quickly from the sofa with one hand stretched out as if in the act of arresting the irrevocable closing of a door. Wait! she cried out. Wait! You have to listen!

"I'm not going to let them destroy him. I'm not going to let anybody destroy him," she said out loud, and she stood looking around the room, bewildered now that she was on her feet and speaking: looking in fumbling surprise at her mother sitting by the fire with her face raised in offense, and at the vet jerking on the chair's edge, his head lowered as he watched the filth caking dry on the carpet under his shoes. She did not turn to look at Candy sitting behind her on the sofa now, but only at the forces mustered there against them, these two other faces and two bodies, and haltingly, separately, at the different pieces of furniture, the logs burning in the fire, the Dresden figures dancing, as if seeing for the first time what they were. "I don't believe it's something incurable," she said, the heavy, subtly glazed eyes moving off from the faces to object after object, and groping, object by object, as if through darkness, back to the faces again. "Nobody can make me believe you can't cure it if you take the care and trouble."

"There's nothing to stop us from having an opinion down from London," the vet began saying without raising his head. He sat there, bowed forward over his soiled pin-striped riding-breeches, with his arms resting on the cloth drawn tight across his legs. While he talked he wove his blunt big fingers in and out, the knuckles rubbing one against the other, and looked down as if in shame at the mud-splattered calves of his tan leather gaiters. "I'd be the first one to say hold off until we get another opinion. I say it's a clear and simple retinitis, come on maybe after influenza although I'd never have judged him convalescent when Mr. Lombe brought him in two months ago. It's the retina worked loose and the sight goes like that, sudden, and if you don't know to the contrary the history of eye-weakness may go right back through his blood. But I say have another opinion in and that would ease it up all 'round for us. Destroying a horse like that isn't anybody's Bank Holiday," he said.

"Ah," said Mrs. Lombe patiently, evenly, "there it is." She did not look at the vet but into the fire's depths for resolution, watching with calm, man-like resignation the uncertainly flickering flame; but still it was to the vet, the only other of sanity's disciples in the room, she spoke. "In-breeding may very well come to be the tragedy of the country before we know it," she said. "Look at our best dogs now, flying off the mouth with hysteeria because of being in-bred generation after generation. They say you're safe if you put a mother to her son or a father to his daughter, but to keep off in-breeding from own brothers and sisters or even first cousins. But where do general rules ever get you? Here's this hunter out there with a history of eye-weakness, a double history if you look at his in-breeding, and nobody," she said but she did not look at her husband, "would have touched him with a yardstick if they'd taken the trouble to run his pedigree out and had him up to pass the vet. I'm not advocating the general importation of foreign dogs or foreign sires, but a great deal of good might be done by bringing in fresh blood pretty freely from the Dominions." Sit down, Nan, you look a fool standing up there, she did not say out loud, but the girl looked in sudden numb bewilderment from side to side a moment and then sat hesitatingly down. At once and for the first time turning and looking at her face, the father reached out and took his daughter's hand. "I think there should decidedly be a feeling of patriotism brought into it," the mother said, and now the sight of them sitting so hand in hand, drawn closer to each other on the sofa but sitting as invulnerable and grave as statues or wax figures roused her to hot, inexplicable fury. She felt the heat flaming in her face and she pushed back in irritation from the fire, thinking that words like patriotism, and thoroughbred, and blood—a horse's good quick blood—should flay them if there were any natural feeling in them. "This country is the home of the thoroughbred, my father used to say," she said, looking towards the vet's stooped horseman's shoulders and his warped strong horseman's legs in the puttees. "You probably know of him by reputation, you may have heard of Major Husen around Chelton," she said, "although he was before your time. I've often wondered if a man not English born and bred can have any gift or sense for horses." She did not look towards her husband but at the vet still who raised his head uncertainly and looked at her and parted his lips and did not speak but swallowed, the skin of his throat permanently and brightly flushed and covered with stubble as white as a sow's. "Major Husen—your grandfather, Nan," she added in stern arrogative rebuke, "he fought year after year against the exporting of our good classic blood, fought it tooth and nail, in season and out, until he was seventy-odd. He'd go up regularly to the sales and try to keep our classic winners on this side of the water by any means he could, and a dozen or more times he did it. On winter nights at home, he spent his time going through the Stud-book until he as good as knew the whole thing by heart. He knew them as well as if they were horses out of his own stables, those leading sires and the sound mares who shouldn't, for the country's sake, be lost to foreign studs." She shifted around completely from the fire, her knees spread still, and looked at them, the father and the daughter, with proud, bold, but hopelessly defeated eyes. "He kept Navan Flyer from going to the Argentine one year, and the next he kept Phronella from being lost to Germany. He wasn't afraid to stand up there and tell them what he thought!" she said, the proudly and pathetically lifted head and the tongue in her mouth scoring them unsparingly for what was weakness and womanliness far worse than sentiment that kept them sitting silent on the sofa, holding hands. "He brought Peace-maker home himself for his own stud, and the speech he made at the sales was printed everywhere. 'Tempting offers, especially from foreigners,'" she quoted him with the exact testy and gallant flavor of disvaluation for the foreigner's name, "'must naturally seem difficult to refuse, but thank God there is one Englishman at least of patriotic sentiment among you, and thank God one Englishman's determination is enough to keep a good horse on its native sod!'"

(One summer, maybe it was the time Candy came home drunk after buying the horned cattle when he was supposed to have bought the Galloways or the Red Polls, I was up-stairs in bed, maybe I was ten or eleven then, and Candy went out from down below and laid down on the lawn in the dark. That was the first time I climbed out the window and crossed the veranda roof and slid down the drainpipe, and the stars were out but it was dark and I couldn't see well, but I knew he was lying there near the hedge, perhaps because other times, earlier, months back or years back, I knew he'd laid out there even if I'd never seen him; perhaps in my sleep I'd heard him year after year when he was drunk open the downstairs door and go out and then re-membered afterwards, like in a dream, the times he'd done it. I had no slippers or anything but my nightgown on and I kept out of the window's lights lying yellow on the lawn and ran over the gravel and the grass to where he was stretched on his back near the hedge, rolling a little from side to side with his hands over his face and moaning. Mother was sitting inside the house, I know she was sitting inside and knitting although I didn't see her, and the wire-less was playing, and perhaps Candy didn't see me there but anyway he knew someone was sitting near him on the grass and he began saying in a low crying voice: "I want my wife. I want my real wife. I want my young little wife to come out and take care of me and save me from what I am. I want her now, my poor thin dying little wife, to start walking up the mountains with me the way she did and not be able to get any further and have to sit down and have to lie down on the pine-needles with me. I want her, I want her," the voice maybe she herself had never heard crying and moaning into his hands. "Out there dying young and living in a house with balconies built in the sun for the dying," he said not to me but to anybody who was sitting there on the cold grass in the dark beside him. "They'd built a café-bar across the road where the dying could get to it easy; before you were dead, you could get down the hall and cross over the road if nobody saw you and get up on a stool if you had enough strength left to do it, and get a drink down or a couple of drinks so later that night you wouldn't meet death too sober." He began shaking with crying now, his shoulders and his raised arms and his body shaking, and his face covered over tight with his hands as he rolled around on the grass. "I used to sit waiting for her there," he said in a moment, "watching the bed on the balcony on the other side of the road for her to be lying on it, and watching the café door for her to come in, and watching the snow on the mountains all summer, waiting and watching like a crazy man for her, my poor little girl, my poor dead dying young wife."

This was the story I had never heard before and I sat shaking with cold in my nightdress and listening to it, holding my teeth tight in my mouth and shaking because now

I knew I wasn't anything to him; there'd been this woman once, this girl, this other wife and none of us knew about her, and now he was drunk he was taking the skeleton out of her bed and out of her grave and hanging these rags of memory on her. I wasn't his child any more because I hadn't been hers, I was nobody, sharing nothing with them, I was just anybody sitting there not far off in the dark for him to say it over and over to. When I thought of her, I set my teeth in the side of my hand to stop their shaking, crying half for her and the other half for what I'd once thought I was to him before I knew about her. "What are you crying for?" he said in a minute, and he had taken his hands away from his face now and was looking towards me although he couldn't have seen me in the dark, only the blurred white nightdress and my knees drawn up and my arms held tight around them. "You haven't anything to cry for. You haven't lost anything," he said, and I said, yes, I've lost something, holding my teeth clenched and not making any sound, I lost something I thought I had. He said the story over and over until I could have repeated it without changing a word or written it down exactly in a copy book, even then that first night I heard it knowing how he must have looked coming up the mountain road that August with his sketch box, and how she looked, the thin young woman standing on the balcony of the sanatorium built there for the ill seeing him for the first time and letting a small bright green feather from a boa or a feather-duster blow down because she wanted him to look up and smile. I sat in my nightgown crying, setting my teeth in the side of my hand and crying in the darkness for her beauty and her affliction and her death.

Now he lay without moving, saying the rest of it to me, and for a long time I couldn't understand. "I lost her," he said. "You never knew her young and ill. You knew somebody who came a long time after that." There were the five or six years in between after he'd married her and after he'd stopped painting the pictures and instead took her from one high place to another and into sanatoriums and out; until I began seeing she hadn't died, she couldn't have died because they cured her: the money she had, a lot of money from her father who'd bred horses, or else marrying for love, or else giving birth to the child who sat listening in the dark curing her for life so that she could take it up where her father had left off and go on breeding horses on the land. And Candy turned over on his face again and lay with the side of it against the grass. "Once in a while," he went on saying, his speech thick from the drink still, "just once in a while when she wakes up in the morning or sometimes when she's reading alone in a room, there's something left, something about her neck or her wrist or the way her hair grows, but otherwise she might just as well have died. Can you understand what I'm saying?" he said, his voice drifting off to sleep or stupor in the darkness. "Can you understand what I'm trying to say? If she hadn't wanted to come back here and live in this country there might never have been the two of them, I mean the one I knew first and the one you didn't, and the other one sitting inside the house now. Sometimes when I come home and see her, when I've had something to drink or the light's not good I see my dead young wife sitting there in the room and I walk quietly so I won't frighten her off and I put my arms around her before she has time to turn around and start talking to me, and before I have to learn it again," he said, the words coming slowly across the grass as the drunken, the flagging, drugged lament drifted hypnotically now towards sleep. "I've learned it over and over and I don't want to have to learn it any more, that there isn't any youth and age, there's only life and death," he said.)

Now he looked up from the sofa at them, looked brightly and pleasantly at his wife beyond the Dresden figures on the table, and at the vet whose lowered face watched in blank bewitchment the slow foul havoc wreaked on the carpet by his shoes. Candy Lombe might have been just the bright, fresh-skinned and well-dressed little man sitting holding to his daughter's hand still, his nose short, pretty and narrow at the nostrils, the mouth soft under the just beginning to lighten trim mustache: except for the eyes shaped long to the temples and uncannily weighted with the nameless and unarticulated dream.

"Well, now the thing is we must all try to be as reasonable as we can about this," he said, looking brightly, almost socially at his wife. It might be he had met her at tea just that day and was putting his best foot forward. "Naturally little Nancy here wants to have everything possible done before we come to a definite decision about Brigand. I think Penson's suggestion about—"

"But a blind horse, a horse incurably blind," the mother began, but now as if instead of looking across the Dresden china dancers at her Candy had spoken her name, or spoken a particular name which they had used a long time ago and in another country and in its deepest signification, she ceased speaking.

"How would you like it!" the girl suddenly cried out.

"What would you feel like if sometime when you were ill they'd wanted to—" She sat on the sofa, not looking at anyone but savagely down at the dark stuff of her skirt, her face white, her teeth biting the wild shuddering sound of crying in. "What if just because you couldn't see any more, or couldn't eat any more, or—or—if you hadn't the strength any more to swim—or climb a mountain without—without losing your breath and having—having to stop and sit down —what if—"

"Hush, Nancy," said Candy softly. "Hush, Nancy," holding to the stiff relentless hand.

"What if you were ill once and nobody—nobody happened to come along and take care of you," the strained gulping voice went on, "just said 'put a bullet through where the brains are,' how would you like dying, how would anybody like dying when they're young and not ready for it yet! When you were ill and young sometime, maybe you wouldn't have been ready," she said, with the tears beginning to come down her face but still not looking at anyone, "just because older people said you were incurable and it was better to shoot you, you wouldn't have wanted it just because people who didn't care any more said it was the kindest—"

"Hush, Nancy, hush," said Candy, stroking her hand.

The vet stood up now and cleared his throat and took his watch from his waistcoat pocket and looked at its face, then slipped it back again.

"If you decide on wanting me to ring up London," he said, buttoning his jacket over with his big, blunt, fumbling fingers, and Mrs. Lombe said:

"You've been extraordinarily patient with us, Mr. Penson. We'll let you know what decision we—" She was standing now, tall and soft, the eyes a little haggard on him. "I don't suppose you'd know what the fee of a London vet might be for running down?" she asked him.

Chapter Four

A T THE end of the week the two things came: the vet called down from London and from London as well the letter from the Irishman. After all these months the letter came saying he was back from Spain, ten days back with a wound in his arm, and he would like to see her but he didn't know if the address would do still or if she had said Nancy Lombe or Nellie that afternoon. "You said at Mrs. Paddington's in Florence you might be back this summer, so I'm taking the chance that you'll remember me," he wrote, and Miss N. Lombe across the envelope outside in a shy quick nervous hand. The letter was folded in her jersey pocket, doubled over and the corners held tight and sharp in her fingers when they followed the London vet out and down the drive, the gravel fresh, wet underfoot where the rain had been that morning, holding onto it as if the mere fact of its paper inflexibility would be enough to hold to no matter what was said. The mother and the London vet walked slightly in advance and Candy was in the house still, having called through the bathroom door: "Nancy, your old pater's still at his ablutions," his voice amplified by the depth of water in the tub and the echoing tiles sounding wondrously strong and clear. "I'll be along when I'm done," he said, and the sound of water gushed into space. He did not say aloud or articulate it even to his own soft naked body bending into the bath:

I will not walk down that road and into the stable and hear it, but will evade it here muffled in shaving lather as fragrant as the springtime. He did not say: I am afraid to go.

The London vet was no longer the country thing but had become a prosperous, aging man like the accepted figure of capitalism in a political cartoon: there were the well-packed jowls and the paunch and the backs of the hairy, dimpled hands. He went at once into the hunter's stall, the breath ticking in congestion through his nose, and there he forced the lids up from the eyes, first one lusterless blank pearl bulging an instant between his thumbs and then the other while the horse's head lifted sightlessly and warily away. The yellow fall of sunny misty heat poured through the box's window onto the vet's graying hair and onto his spectacles' glass while he said, not to the horse's concepts or perceptions but still in his intuitive hearing: "The poor chap will have to be put down." He looked into the hunter's set milky eye and said the local man could do the trick as he himself had not come prepared to do it. And the mother standing on the oaten bedding said they had promised to give the owner time to decide, they had promised to wait a little. "My daughter," she said of the girl standing out of sight behind him and behind the horse holding to the letter in her pocket and hearing the man's breath clogging in his nose, the thing continuing as they had read of it in textbooks: if there was any doubt in the marksman's mind or if it was to be done by a novice, a line should be drawn in chalk on the horse's forehead from the right ear to the center and from the left ear to the center and a crossline drawn down where they conjoined. "I don't see why it has to be done, I don't see why," the girl said, her voice coming suddenly hoarse and tragic and young out of the stable's shadow.

The vet did not quite turn around to see her when he said the place to aim for and hit was the exact intersection of the chalk lines, the unmistakable center of the frontal bone between the eyes. "No," the girl said, this time only half aloud. "No." She thought This is the illusion and the real time is night, and the condition not waking protest because I am lying in bed asleep with this letter held under the pillow in my hand. The vet is not breathing like that through his nose, but it is my own breathing. I am lying in bed asleep and these are the monsters of childhood: the reptile disguised as authority in dark blue wool with dandruff on his shoulders, the shape my mother has taken now the monument erected to all childhood fear. I am saying "no, no, no" in my sleep and they cannot hear me. The smell of hay and horse is memory and the light is cool and blurred like just-remembered light while the tide of breathing rises and ebbs, rises and ebbs with the strange deep machinations of the heart in sleep. If you cannot give sight to a horse, not only to this horse but any horse, to the finest grandest pedigreed champion of them all, you hand it death like a third eye through the forelock, you give it its peep at paradise through one small black-lipped hole. You do this for the horse, not for the owner nor for the world, but for the bony, mysteriously limbed and soft-mouthed beast who is stumbling in silent panic from darkness to darkness. You shatter his brow at one stroke for him the way a strong man's fist shatters the frail panels of a door to let in the light, and the constant dream of nothing in his inconstant world of rippling skin, twitching shoulder, flicking ear splinters like glass splintering loud at night. You are awake, Brigand, toss your mane. The dream of blindness has ceased, darling. You are no longer sightless, you are dead. "No!" she cried out, putting her knuckles to her teeth. "No! They won't do it! I won't let them do it!"

She ran panting, gasping, not crying yet, out the stable door and up the drying, softly steaming gravel to the house. Behind her the talk went on, armed now with a capable relentless pity: get grooms, the local vet, the huntsman to tell her their experiences with horses gone blind or crippled horses, get her a book on it that will give her the proper viewpoint. If it's her horse, then let the matter go a day or two until she's understood the thing in and out: the mercy first and then the necessity of it. Tell her you can't teach a horse to accept blindness because his world is sight, and in a while she'll come around all right, she'll see the humaneness in doing it as soon as it can be done. Ah, that she'll have to do for all our sakes; we're not a hospital here for the maimed and we need the place for the work I'm trying to get on with against odds. Against God, almost, but anyway against man who was still locked behind the bathroom door and whistling.

"Just coming!" he called out when the girl struck the door with her hand. "Just coming, Nancy!"

She leaned in despair on it in the instant before he opened it to her: first hearing the whistling cease, and then the key turn, and then she saw him there, his lips puckered up to begin the tune again but his eyes through the bathroom's haze recoiling from disaster into their own queer dream-drugged blue. His hands were lifted to smooth the bay rum onto his hair, the sleeves of toweling slipping back on his full womanish arms to the dimpled elbows, and she flung herself wild and crying against him.

"They'll do it if you don't stop them! They're going to do it if you don't stop them!"

The tears stopped suddenly at the sound of her own voice saying what was true. But it was only for a little while she believed strength could be given or taken, given by Candy or any man, or taken from the Irishman's letter. She began seeing how it was now as a savage might have seen it and made a picture of it with berry stains, or some coloring as primitive, or stitched it toughly in beads or thread on cloth: the small helpless lone island of the self out of voice's call or swimmer's reach lying among the scattered inaccessible islands of those other selves. In the three nights that came after with the horse still living and the Irishman written to, she saw that unpeopled landscape and the vast waters washing forever unspanned between the separate islands, and she touched the bones in bed with her, the bones of the shoulder, the arm, the hand, and the thigh's bones lying tenacious in her flesh, and the skull's inexorability underneath the hair. If there is any strength it is in these, it is here, not in running fast to Candy for help or in writing Dear Mr. Sheehan: It was jolly nice to have a letter from you and I hope you're wound is getting on well. I'm feeling very bad because the London vet we called down here says they'll have to destroy my horse. My father said to suggest for you to come down here one afternoon and he would be glad to meet you at the station. I know you said you knew horses, so maybe . . . lying awake at night in bed and saying over again these words that had been written down on paper and would be read on paper, she thought of the horse's unwritten, unrecorded, uncommitted world of sight and hearing, touch and smell, the horse's moving world of myriad credulous sensation, and lying so night after night the line came clearer through sleeplessness and through the room's dark until its clarity became the impulse to get up and walk with bare feet to the open window and repeat it aloud: "The horse is frightened by the bush because the bush unexpectedly turns and waves a branch."

She put her jersey on but she could not find her slippers at once in the darkness so she climbed over the window-ledge without them and crossed the veranda roof and slid down the drainpipe with the cotton nightdress drawn tight between her legs. It was warm, for once here in England Italian-warm, even the grass warm under her feet as she crossed the corner of the lawn. Because of the bite of the gravel she kept to the grass and beds, going quickly towards the stable, and at the drive's curve she left the soft clipped border and ran painfully and rapidly across. No man, no woman, no girl, no Irishman, no doctor, vet, science, no kind of human knowledge can save him or give his sight back to him, she thought shouldering the door aside; he'll stand there shaking with palsy and funk in that state of incurable blindness and incurable terror until they put him down. She walked barefoot across the stable floor to where he was, and opened the door of his stall in the dark and spoke his name to him. "Brigand," she said out loud, and without seeing it she felt the shudder of fear and anguish that washed down him but he did not shift, perhaps not knowing whether to shift to right or left to let her by. There was no light, only the smell of horse and the taste of sweet clean-kept horse in the air, and she heard his stablemate rousing and moving in her stall beyond. So you'll stand there day after night, night after day, not knowing one from the other until your time's up, she said. She could feel him strong as stone but living as she shoved past him in the stall. You'll stand here, what's in you rearing for death and shaking with fright unless you listen to me. She drew his head down in the curve of her arm, firmly, almost without tenderness. Let the bush unexpectedly turn and touch your flank so you'll get the slap of its leaves like that without sight when the bush turns, she tried saying, and then she began it again: Your eyes, my friend, have clotted in your head. However, the road still flows away under the feet, the fence still bucks under you when you gather up your legs to rise, the house still pivots in the garden showing first one angle and then the other to you, the hedges have not ceased to pour by like water, the trees have never stopped waltzing, the clouds careening. It is you, my steed, who must comprehend motion without sight's limitations as long as we have dispensed with sight. Let the bush slap you full in the face and you will acknowledge its presence the same way as you did when you saw it unexpectedly turn and wave a branch.

The first night she took him out onto the drive only, leading him slowly by the head-rope through the dark. There were no stars, no wind, and the evergreens were a little wet still from the day's rain as they passed under, and the leaves of the wayfaring tree and the laurel brushed light and wet across their faces. It was after one o'clock, perhaps just on two but no bells in the village below, as there would have been in Italy, to say it, and the girl walked near him, her shoulder moving against the hunter's shoulder as they walked. She said Next time I'll wear slippers, damn it, stepping in pain on the gravel, and now with the great unseeing and unseen beast moving diffidently beside her she began the scheming: "She said they'd let me have two weeks. Because of Candy, she gave me the two weeks. I'll listen to Penson explaining it over again, and I'll hear the grooms out, and I'll read the book. But she's given me two weeks to prepare for death. That's always that. In a fortnight anything can happen."

The third night she put the bit between his teeth and the bridle on him, and on the fourth she took him down past the lower edge of the paddocks and along the path by the stream. Here the way was narrow and they went single file, the girl ahead and the horse coming after on his rein, and where the bank lowered she led him towards the water, saying aloud: "If I know this place in the dark without being able to see it any more than you can, you can believe in it too, you can reconstruct the picture out of chaos and memory's ruins," but the horse stood back, the strong, the monstrously night-magnified body halted and the head raised in bewildered innocence. "Come," she said, "come," and now the sudden jerk as she kicked her slippers off did not startle him as it had the night before when they came to grass. "Come, my man, come," she said, and she gathered the reins up beneath the quivering pendent lip. She stooped, holding him still, and in one hand raised a palmful of water to his nostrils and wet his mouth. "Smell it," she said, "smell water," and now the forefoot advanced with her, and now the other, until the stream washed across his hoofs. She paused with him in the running water, feet on the slippery submerged stones, and he stretched his neck out and then brought his head down, as the rein slackened, to the smell and murmur and the touch of water, and she heard him begin to drink. She put her hand under his cheek and felt the windpipe pull and tauten, and felt in his throat the strong passage of the water, irresistibly and powerfully channeled like the passage of electric current through his neck and jaws. In a moment she said "come" to him again, and they crossed through the stream together, the cold washing to their knees, and reached the sedges and waded through them and clambered up to land. "So you see," she said aloud, and she led him on under the beeches to where the trees grew the thickest and took him in through the underbrush, her bare feet shrinking sideways with pain, but still taking him fiercely through it. First the road that first night, she thought, and after that the grass and the water, and now the trees and what's tripping him up underfoot to say Nothing has gone, blind horse, nothing has altered. When they were through it she stopped again at the edge and drew the mayblossom branches down over his face, gently drawing them down and gently letting them brush upward like veils of some inexplicable substitute for sight. That night she took him back by the marsh where by day the yellow iris could be seen growing, and he did not falter but sought his way with her through the invisible fragrant lilies in the dark.

All day he would stand in the loose box with the mare or a filly for company two stalls away, curried and groomed and the place done out from under him, and the cat coming in through the window and rubbing along his leg. By day he was this thing, the prisoner, the condemned man in the death cell on the final stretch of living, not of a species to play cards and smoke the last cigarettes with the guards while he waited, but silently, motionlessly, completely waiting. But at night the stable door moved back and the latch of the stall gate was lifted and he moved out in blindness and wonder with her into the slowly reconstituted, slowly redeemed and infinite world; until the night came when she did not pick up the reins and bring them forward across his head to turn him in the stall and guide him across the stable out into the insect-murmurous dark. It was the sixth or seventh night and once he was bridled she pushed past him and opened the stall gate and standing alone on the stable floor she said, "Come on, handsome," the voice casual enough, but as she waited there in the stable's complete obscurity her heart began to tremble. She held her hands down fast by her sides, her eyes were closed tight as fists in her face, and she stood scarcely daring to hear the confused stamp of the hoofs seeking position as he turned, not hearing actual sound any more but seeming to hear what might come if he fumbled and missed the narrow way out. It might have been hours—it was less than a minute—before he was clear of the stall and his nostrils came seeking the air for her, the hoofs' sound having altered from their stroke on straw-muffled brick to their thud on timber, and then he lipped her shoulder. "It's as black as your hat," she said as she took him across the threshold's beam. "I can't see any more than you can." She was shaking hard, as if in the teeth of cold.

The Irishman wrote back at once, gravely beginning it "Dear Miss Lombe," and she showed the letter to Candy. "He can't come down on account of his arm, on account of the dressings," she said. Candy had been by the morning bus to Pellton and bought two detective stories in paper covers at Woolworth's shop in Fore Street, and he sat on the veranda in the fan-backed Indian armchair reading *Wanton Killing* in mild, soft-shaven, immaculately accoutred peace (because this would kill the hours of the afternoon and a portion of the evening, this story that did not for an instant deal with people but with the familiarly stamped counterfeits of detective, family, doctor, corpse). On the corner of the ping-pong table lay the other, *Murder in Hand*, still clean and marvelously unread (instrument lying in readiness to slug tomorrow afternoon and evening in their turn into timeless insensibility). "He says he'd like to meet you, Candy, but he can't come down," the girl said, "but look, turn the page," and she turned it for him. "Look what he says about horses." The climbing roses, their leaves and new buds even mildewed by the weather, grew meagerly about them, reaching unblooming up the rusted trelliswork. The afternoon was gray and still, a warm, heavy, iron-dull day with the hawthorn and maples on the lawn standing motionless against it. The single bees that sailed loudly to the laboriously-opening black clots of rose were as incongruous as humming birds boring for succulence in granite flowers. Candy put his detective story face down and open on the end of the ping-pong table and looked at the letter he held in his hand.

" 'I've often seen and ridden horses with "wall" eyes, cataracts (very common), horses blind in one eye, and I've known one or two cases where hunters have been totally blinded by accident. They were not destroyed, though, but put onto farm work, where—' " He stopped reading it aloud, thinking If he did come down I'd meet him at the station, either at Monkton Junction or Eastleigh, and if he came by the late train the pub would be open and over a drink we might get somewhere and for that half hour, in the process of getting somewhere, we'd talk like men. Just for that half hour before we got back here to the house we would be two men talking together, until he saw me for what I am, the one flaw, the single mistake, mistaken as the futile, idle, the evasive must be mistaken in a décor of rearing, stamping, accoupling activity; and as the penniless out of their place and in disguise once unmasked are the mistaken. If he comes down, for a little while my clothes (so much like other men's) will see me through and my receptive manner, for the first half hour over the first drink they'll do; and then he'll see the murder book and the shiftless hours in which no one comes to me, no subordinate or equal, for authority or permission, and at last he'll see the empty glass under the chair.

"Go on," the girl said. "Read the rest of it," and Candy, thinking of murder book and empty glass as weapon and insignia, went on reading aloud:

" 'They were not destroyed, though, but put onto farm work, where they did very well. I don't know anything about retinitis.' " The mother came out through the dining-room door onto the veranda's stone, the basket with the trowel and fork in it on her forearm, and her old gardening gloves pulled on her hands. She paused as if the roses and not the words had stopped her, and touched the blighted leaves with the gardening scissors' beak. " 'I imagine it's not a very common affliction,' " Candy's voice went on. " 'All I know is that the retina's that part at the back of the eye which aches when we come suddenly from darkness into light.' "

"Who's this?" said the mother in a light, inconsequential tone. She stood like a stranger near them under the stricken rose vines, her eyes the perceptive, conjecturing eyes of the human meeting, or only seeking vainly to meet, the cold, unearthly vision of their wide, glazed eyes. The father looked up and cleared his throat and smiled with a sudden little show of daring under his small neat mustache.

"Oh, that's Mr. Sheehan," he said brightly. "Mr. Sheehan calling all stations."

"Who's Mr. Sheehan?" the mother said and she smiled rather bitterly at the dark riddled leaves.

"He's Irish," said Candy, turning the page of the letter as if the actual stamp of his nationality might be set there for the eye to see. "A broth of a boy—"

"I met him in Florence," the girl said. She stood quite still by the ping-pong table, her eyes stopped motionless, her lips ceased moving, her hands and the bare white slender forearms hanging absolutely quiet from the gray jersey's elbow sleeves. I know nothing about her now, nothing, the mother thought bitterly. She looked across, seeking to find and focus the gaze of her daughter's eyes, thinking Ah, yes, here I am as you see me, the old woman who can't think back that far any more, the commander of the ship that would have floundered if I hadn't stepped into the male boots and buckled on the male regalia, an old woman going to fat now in the permanently borrowed paraphernalia that a man, not a woman, should wear.

"That's quite interesting, but you don't have to be sulky about it," she said aloud.

"I'm not sulky," the girl said, and in spite of herself she began to tremble, not only the bones and the flesh but the very marrow shaking and crumbling in her. There was no gooseflesh on her bare hanging arms, but she felt her heart, her substance quaking in her and her teeth chattering in her head. "He knows a lot about horses. He says blind horses don't have to be put down."

"Yes, you are sulking," said the mother, and her hand with the gardening shears in it trembled too. "You've been up to something; now you know you've been up to something you don't want me to know about, Nan."

"He says blind horses can be put onto farm work, so if a blind horse can be put onto work, then I can ride mine, I can teach him," the girl said. She stood looking motionlessly, quietly beyond, beyond her mother and past the lawn, beyond the day even to that irresistible goal perhaps weeks or months ahead, almost visually perceiving the plane of victory on which the horse would pound homeward sightless, outstripping the clear-eyed thoroughbreds, taking the obstacles higher, the ditches wider. "I know I could teach mine," she said, trembling before the still imperfect vision of the truth. "I could take him out a little bit every day, a little bit more all the time—"

The mother reached over and took the Irishman's letter out of Candy's hand and she said:

"I won't have you riding a blind horse and killing yourself and the poor beast. Thank God, there's a more humane way of putting it down—"

"Brigand's a He," said the girl. "He's a man. You might speak of him like that."

"It's a gelding," said the mother. "There's no need to

flatter it with a sex." She turned the three pages of Mr. Sheehan's letter and she said: "He's found time to write you a lot of nonsense, this young gentleman of yours," and in that oddly patient and at the same time oddly grieving voice, her thumb in the split leather, mud-whitened and caked glove holding the sheet, she read the sentences on the last page out. " 'It is easier to change an animal's receptivity of the world abruptly because in his two-dimensional existence everything enters from the outside. For animals a new sun rises every morning and a new morning comes with every dawning day. It is only human reasoning which insists that it is the same sun rising or the same moon waning. That is where Rostand did not understand the psychology of "Chantecler." The cock could not think that he woke up the sun by his crowing. To him the sun does not go to sleep, it goes into the past.' * He is quite an intellectual, your Mr. Sheehan," said the mother, speaking without rancor as if she knew and accepted the end of the story now. " 'So you can quite naturally and I should think with comparative ease give your horse a new world of action by giving him a new discernment for the motions which go on around him. I think this is what you meant, or rather what—' " Suddenly the mother broke off her reading and flicked the letter back to Candy where he sat in the fan-backed chair. "This sort of business isn't going to get us anywhere," she said.

"Come now," said Candy, and he smiled at them both with the same little jerk of summoned courage as before. "From the point of view of that horse costing us anything,

* P. D. Ouspensky, *Tertium Organum*, rev. ed., Knopf, 1922.

if I started in giving up my good tobacco, you know, and my cigars, and stuck to that kind of pipe fodder that makes my head go round, it ought to pay for that chap's food and drink for some months to come." His round neat little chin was lifted clear of his shirt's soft collar and the pale blue knitted tie and his hands held fast to the wicker arms of the chair. "I don't want Nancy to ride him, no, that I don't want," he said. "I don't want to have Nancy stumbling around on a blind horse, but I say let her have him for this summer anyway. She can take him walking up and down the drive if she wants him as badly as all that, Nan. This Irish chap here, this boy Sheehan, he seems to know—"

"Ah, your incurable softness, yours and Nan's incurable false softness," said the mother in a low bitter voice. She looked at his short, helpless hands hanging from the sleeves of the squire's jacket, the nails rounded clean and white on the childlike fingers that held to the chair's arms, and the empty glass put aside carefully beneath the chair. "Keep that animal rotting in blindness out there all the summer? What sort of sentimentality is it? For his health's sake, any horse must have his work-out, but you'd keep him closed out there with a step or two up the drive every day, and you'd break his heart and spirit for him! If you go on, you two," she said, holding onto the anger, "I'll put that crazy horse down myself, with my own hand I'll do it because I'm the only one here who'd have the compassion to do it—"

By the tenth day it was hot, a complete heat had descended on the country and the moon rose clearly at night. At supper Mrs. Lombe said they were leaving the yearlings out all night in the upland pastures, and thinking or dreaming of this the girl awoke as she always awoke now soon after midnight, quickly and without interruption rousing night after summer night as if someone entered the room at the specified hour and touched her arm and said it was time to come. She thought at once of the yearlings out in the grass, and she got up and put on her slippers and her jersey and crossed to the open window on the veranda roof. If they're out he has the right to go up there and graze near them and talk to them across the rails, or even go so far as . . . Or even go loose a while with them, the yet unthought, unspoken thing was shaping; not with the colts, she came near to establishing it as intention as she crossed the grass and the flower-beds to the stable. The colts play as wild as cats together, but the fillies are gentle, she thought, not quite coming to it as she shouldered back the stable door.

They went out the drive, and this time turned up the road towards the stud-farm, the horse waiting while she opened the pale painted gate and then following when she spoke his name. The main buildings stood on the rise ahead, bright white under the moon: the brood-mares' boxes looking south down the pasture-land, the granaries and the men's sleeping quarters to the north, and the stud-groom's cottage nearer, white under its thatch, standing to the right of the road. She thought I used to think jockeys and grooms never married, as if they weren't like men or anyway not whole men, just pieces of men cut down like that to fit a horse, but there's the stud-groom married and sleeping with his wife now behind those windows. I used to think of them all as something less than men because something more, like immortals, jockeys and grooms and huntsmen and vets, but whatever they say now I know better. I'm going to ride my horse, perhaps not tonight or tomorrow night but in the end I'm going to ride him. They came up out of the shadow of the firs and beeches, coming out of the trees' exactly defined darkness and walking into the open moon-whitened country like walking into the light of day. The home buildings and the cottage were white as bone, the fields, the moon-dappled pasture, the blackthorn hedges wrapped in stillness as they came past them, the girl and the horse keeping to the grass for quiet and their footfalls muffled as they passed the closed windows and moved out again into the open country, the two survivors moving through a bleached plague-stricken land.

Close to the buildings lay the small enclosures where the mares were turned out at once after foaling, and near by them the brood-mares' paddocks, longer, ampler, but likewise with the house standing between them and the north. Stretching farther afield (even in childhood she had felt in the sweep of the opening land the conditions of youth and its frenzy) were the yearlings' paddocks, acre on acre reaching out of sight to the orchards' drop. Far below, unseen, unheard, almost out of the moon's reach, the stream ran on. The paddocks set close to the home buildings stood empty under the wide night's light, for the mares and their foals were closed in until the dew would be off the grass in the morning: within the walls they were one still, mare and foal, mare and foal in their boxes, still sharing the same fodder-fragrant and straw-fragrant air. For a little while longer foal and dam pressed body to body, moved out in the early morning limb to limb, the mother sleeping now with her head lowered and the child with his legs bent under him, folded close, and his nose resting vulnerably on the trampled hay. Weaning time had not come yet and the child still flaunted his willful, wayward lip and eye, his glossy belly propped on stilts, for a little while longer drew milk from her, drank from the same wood bucket, licked the same salt stone. It would come, wax to its peak of sorrow, then wane like the wooing-season: they would be taken from each other, foal from dam, and dam from foal, and for two days they would not eat but run the length of the paddock rails seeking each other and calling out, while the pain numbed slowly and at last died wholly in their flesh. For two more days they would stand with their eyes set on nothing but the memory of each other until the lineaments of that too faded, but when the foal turned down his head to lip the grasses again a part of that fearless, fiery arrogance was gone, already and forever.

The girl and the horse passed by the bright white-painted gates and the posts and rails that marked out the paddocks, following up the road that lay between. And as they walked the colts began coming to the bars and whinnying out to them, first to the sound of footsteps and then to the sight of them passing in the moonlight, and the hunter lifted his head on the rein and turned it towards their high chiming voices. Not here, the girl said and she drew him on; these are the colts and they'd play too hard for you and bruise you, but still the clear foolish voices called out to him to come. It was better than half a mile to the last big paddock where the fillies were turned free on nights like this, and the length of the way the colts ran to the bars and called out after them, running lightly in couples through the

86

moonlit grass. It was only in distances that the moon's power seemed to fail, blotted out in the far maze of firs, myrtles, and the scrub pines grown down the west side against the wind.

At first there were none of the fillies to be seen, lost somewhere in the rich clover down at the meadow's end, or standing asleep in the paddock's eight-acre stretch with their necks curved over one another's. The girl climbed to the top bar of their gate and sat there in the warm, foreign-seeming night, the slippers hanging loose on her bare feet, the short-sleeved jersey undone. "Come," she said, and for an instant he faltered as she drew him forward on the rein, without sight knowing (perhaps because my voice is coming now from above instead of beside him) that the barrier was there. "Come," she said, and now he came carefully forward until the full deep breast came to a pause against the bars. The face hung long and utterly quiet, utterly patient beside her, the long flexible lip seemingly ready to smile if only the gift of humor or whimsy were given, the damp forelock ready to curl in the dew-moist blank soft air. In another while the fillies began coming up the paddock in the moonlight, first one and then another, and now in couples, and now in threes, picking their way like deer with their heads high and their delicate ears tipped forward, until at last the nine of them had come tentatively to the railing, their noses lifted without shyness to lip the smell and substance of horse and human flesh.

None of the men asleep in the home buildings, nor the stud-groom in his cottage heard it, but Apby started suddenly out of sleep remembering the sound of a horse going past on the grass, not running but simply walking quietly by, perhaps in the grass by the roadside. He (who had sought to be a jockey and who had never raced except in country fairs) was dreaming of the colored caps, the striped satin shirts, the narrow pennants flying on the grandstand, and on the fast track of dreams and even through the sound of cheering, he heard the muffled passing of the horse's feet beneath the window. There was no horse in sight by the time he was out of bed and opened the shutters, but still he pulled his trousers on and went down the ladder into the center mixing-room, and unlocked the door and went out onto the road. For a while he stood there waiting to get the sound again, and he heard it, moving farther and farther, fainter and fainter, like two hands clapping slower and farther and fainter, until the sound had ceased completely, and he said There's a horse got loose up by the last paddocks, and he started walking that way.

Chapter Five

BUT AT least he kept the secret, he didn't tell either
the other grooms or the masters because by keeping
quiet about it the trouble over the hunter's age between him and the girl was finished. She was sitting on the
top rail of the gate when he came up the road, and the
fillies were galloping wild in the paddock, the group of
them wheeling together, first one in the lead and then another; and she started talking to him without turning her
head, as if she had expected him to come or just anybody she
could say it to to come and stand there below her, a little
to one side of her, looking over the top bar at the horses
going crazy underneath the moon. She said: "That's my
horse in there with them." She had her hands closed into
fists and she kept beating her left fist up and down on her
knee as she watched them reeling into one corner and out
of it and sweeping wildly down the land. "My horse is in
there running with them, look, he's with the last three, my
blind horse running. . . ."

The fillies came snorting past the rails, their necks and
shoulders leaning to the curve, their manes blowing, and
galloped down the slope towards where the water passed
and out of sight, then up the opposite side of the field
they came like the rush of the wind coming, and the hunter
with them, the tall, stern, bony body stretching and limber-
ing with them as they swung across the grass. She said: "I

89

took his bridle off and opened the gate for him," her hand clenched tight and beating on her knee as she watched them go. "I gave him a crack and he went straight in to them. I've won," she said, not turning her head to him. "I won against them all, even against you, Apby. I won."

He stood bandy-legged and seemingly dwarfed below her, leaning stubbornly on the painted gate, his arms raised and crossed on the top bar and his chin laid on them, almost classless now as he leaned insolently on the bar below her in this place where, at this hour, they had no right to be.

"No, you didn't win, you didn't win nothing at all," he said, leaning casually and boldly there below her. In a while he might take a cigarette out of his breeches' pocket and strike a match to it and stand there smoking without a sav-ing-your-presence or a grant-your-grace and let it hang dry on his lip while he went on saying in the moonlight: "You didn't win because that's nothing you're giving a horse, that's no life for a grown horse, grazing and romp-ing with yearlings, running like that like maybe a hundred blind horses would run with their kind. That don't get 'im anywheres," he said, and she looked quickly down at him, seeing him like a stranger now that for once the brown-and-white checked soiled cap was absent and the hair showed pressed flat from sleep against the skull; seeing the small elfin-profiled face of the doer for horses, the delicate-boned face of the administrator to their flesh, the inevitable steward to their intimacies. She thought Perhaps no one ever with big bones is good with horses, only these half men, while he said: "What have you won if you haven't found his use for 'im? This kind of thing is all right and all that, but it isn't finding his use for 'im."

"But there's no need to destroy him now," she said. "No one on earth'd put a horse down that can run like that. No one alive—"

"What kind of a deal are you giving him at that?" the groom said, his chin resting on his arms on the bar as he watched the galloping horses take the rise. "You're not offering him much by just turning him out to grass for the time he's got to go. I've known a few horses and I say as he'd rather be dead than in the stable and out year in and year out the way he'd be." The horses came head-on towards the gate, then bent their course and swerved like a flock of birds, and bending still chopped short the corner, and the girl's hair lifted in her neck with the wind of their passing and slowly sank again when they were by. "Grass ain't always the 'appy 'ome of rest," Apby said. "You've got the month of June and that's the best here, and after June the flies start driving the horses off their heads, and when it's late September and on the grass has no more taste than paper."

"Because you want him dead," she said, looking straight ahead down the paddock. "You all want it." And now the groom took his arms from the top bar and fished in his breeches' pocket for the cigarette and brought it out and straightened it in his fingers before he put it in his mouth and struck the match and held it, the fire-bright spark of what might have been life itself cupped in his hand's bones an instant while the lowered head, the tilted mouth leaned to it, and the small jaws sucked quickly at the air. "It's all system with you and all the rest of them," the girl was saying, looking at him now and watching him shake the match's flame out and let it drop into the grass. "So many boxes, so much room, so many hands for the work, so—"

"You get him his own work to do and I'll be the first to groom him," he said, folding his arms on the rail again and the cigarette hanging on his arrogant lip. "Make a horse out of him as long as you can't never now make a sire," he said, the humor turned coarse and free as if it were another groom, not girl and not employer, sitting on the gate above him. "You cut out his work for him and I'd be the first to do for him morning, noon, and night," he said, and the girl said quickly:

"I wouldn't let you touch him."

"Saddle 'im, I'd say, saddle 'im," the groom went on saying. He drew sparingly at the cigarette, letting the ash grow, sparingly letting the smoke rise. "He's queer enough for anything I'd ever seen so he'd likely let you do it. Saddle 'im up and give 'im his paces. Put 'im on a Ward Union double-bridle and just try 'im out."

And now the fillies, as if at a given signal, suddenly broke apart near the fence and quietly scattered; gentle as mares and with the same matured wisdom, they shook their manes on their necks and dropped their heads to graze. Only the throbbing flanks and bellies remained as remnant of their senseless wild abandon, and slowly, step by long-drawn lingering step, they moved off eating at the grass. For a moment the hunter was left there in isolation as they went in their separate, lingering directions, his head raised and searching, perhaps seeking sight now that the comprehensible motion of flight had ceased; and then abruptly he sought it no longer. Whether it was the sound of their still hot unsubsided breathing or the pull of their teeth at the grass that came to his ears now and calmed his heart's equivocal panic, the girl watching him from the top of the gate saw him drop his strong long head and begin to crop the herbage as did the others, and move, as did the others, step after prolonged half-arrested step, grazing at peace in the mysteriously shining night.

Two days after that, when she wrote to Mr. Sheehan again, she wrote:

"At first it didn't go very well because as long as I was on his back my horse got panicky and he wasn't sure about stepping on the road. If I got off and led he went all right, or he'd follow me all right, but when I mounted him again it was the same thing. He'd feel out the ground all the time with his forefoot before he'd go, or he'd stop short, maybe thinking there was a hole he couldn't see in front of him. But I managed to get him around the long way by the stream and into the paddock where there weren't any horses out. It's one of the colts' paddocks and it's more than eight acres square. When he remembered he couldn't see he stopped like a shot and that might be bad if you were going fast but maybe he'll get over that too. I'm trying the half-passage with him because I've seen quite a few horses and I don't see any good in just turning him out to grass," came the predication of youthful authority and youthful plagiarism. "I've noticed that turning them out like that isn't always their happy home of rest. There's only the month of June here and after that the flies begin pestering them, and everybody knows autumn grass tastes like paper to them. But a horse is no good to himself or to anybody if he hasn't got a use or any work to do, and training him to obey can give him a use so even if he's blind he can begin living his life again."

So the battle had another aspect to it now, the ranks were a little altered. On the side of death, the marvelously equipped cohorts of extinction, were the mother, the vets, the stud-groom, precedent; and on the other the Irishman nursing his arm up in London and writing to her, and Apby come to heel. Between the two federations Candy erred as a victim of amnesia might have wandered, the meaning of the issue lost in confusion, the name forgotten, only the sense of urgency, perplexed and sketchily defined but present. He stood at the dining-room window in the evening tapping out the verses with his fingertips on the anciently rain-stained glass: Oh, Nancy, Nancy, your doting parent, is afraid circumstances will warrant. Or If ever you took it into your head, to ride a horse that ought to be— Or If you ever rode that crazy hunter—punter, munter, bunter, runter. His fingertips drummed across the glass with the rhythm of what he was making up, seeking a way, if way there was, to establish a truce between will and will without he himself having to make any declaration or come to any choice. Because there must be an end to it he was almost persuaded now that the alternative lay between two deaths: either the hunter's provoked death or the girl's death if she rode him, and the menace of horse seemed imminent, the threat of equine inhuman power seemed ready to cast the dauntless and the daring down and stamp their life out underfoot. He stood tapping his fingers on the pane and watching the evening coming, the mild June evening in which thundered the defiance of the big-necked, the monstrous-thighed and bony-headed beasts who reeled towards growing timber in their madness (he had read of men willfully killed by horses who took trees as the last resort, low boughs or the trunks themselves, to strike their masters from their backs); he could see the vision of them cracking their legs on fences they'd jumped short and crashing gigantically, massive as floundering whales on the defenseless frail bodies of the mounted young; saw them in steeplechase and point-to-point and hunt, the cripplers, the murderers, striking out left and right and beneath them in their folly, the hard-hoofed, hysterical killers breaking their own backs as they fell, a mass of twisted, writhing tonnage, snapping their own necks as they collapsed across the bars on the still incredulous, still fearless young, the dying monsters killing as they died.

"Tum-te-te-tum, tum-te-te-tum, ta-ta," he hummed aloud now as something like actual physical fear began to shake his soul. He thrummed his fingertips on the window and he thought, The best horse story I ever heard was the one about the cavalry regiment galloping hard, four a-breast, up the village street, young sparks in their uniforms making their mounts take it fast to show the population, in particular the female, how they sat the saddle. Ah, but the street was narrow, lads, and ah, but vanity, that fluctuating current that deflects the blood stream in our hearts, was lashing the horse past all endurance: it seemed the eyes must boil from their heads, and their tongues spume from their jaws, and their lungs burst wide and hang in shreds upon their chests' scaffolding, when what happened but a cob and buggy turned out from a cross street and peacefully came towards them, slowly because it was summer and the driver with his feet propped on the dashboard, half asleep. The horses, remember, left six inches free on either side as they came up the village street, their necks at the extremity, their legs stretched reaching for the weapon with which to do the killing; ah, murderers, lusters, gangsters all, see the horse coming slowly and flickeringly, like in one of the first moving pictures, his feet seeming to wave from side to side like slowly waved handkerchiefs as he drew the buggy or else the buggy pushed him down the street, see the blinders on the sides of his face, if you can remember that far back, and the reins hanging slack because the driver had forgotten, just before meeting death, about the briefness of man's allotted span, and see the last touch, the comic feet propped on the dashboard. Towards this familiar (if you were alive in the horse and buggy age) and insignificant (if you did not admit time's aggregation) and helplessly advancing vehicle came the cavalry, unarmed except for haste and heat and savagery, while the buggy's shafts, like spears carried low and wary by African warriors on the trail, took aim in measured preparation.

Damn horses, in the name of youth, God damn them, Candy said, and he turned away from the window to the sight of his wife through the double-doorway, knitting by the silent radio. There were six horses less after that debacle, he told himself with pleasure: one man less, the driver dying with his legs stuck up on the dashboard still like a dead bird's legs sticking straight up in the air, because he didn't wake up in time to choose, or if he had chosen what could he have done with only a couple of yards between him and the galloping horde? But six horses less, two of them run through by the buggy's shafts and their hearts split on the skewers, and four of them with broken shoulders and broken necks trampled to death in headlong panic, six of them less to bolt and rear and stampede, and the officers only badly hurt, only disfigured. She was knitting with pink, and a towel spread over her skirt to keep the delicate wool from soiling, and he thought "badly hurt," how magical, how truly rich and sweet it is, "disfigured" or "badly hurt," the unhoped-for reprieves from death. He sauntered over the worn little islands of the rugs towards his wife, his hands in the pockets of his coat and his neat, well-manicured thumbs out, knitting what? he thought, half-jocularly asking, For God's sake, knitting what? Part of it was humorous and part tender, and part the complete if dimly credited perception that not time itself but the belief that there were lapses in it was the illusion: she might be sitting nearly twenty years back knitting something for Nancy not born yet, the same evening, the same supper, the same twilight outside the windows on which the rain had a long time dried. And at that same time, me beginning what was to be my artistic career, fatherhood the accessory not the keystone to life, envisaging clearly then the now dimmed, wasted features of what was to have been honor and accomplishment year after simultaneous year.

"Nan," he said, coming to the last island on which she sat marooned, "perhaps you ought to be making a confession to me," and he made a gesture with his thumb towards the pale wool and the needles in her hands. She heard the part-jocular, part-tender voice and she looked quickly up at him, at the rather gallant little figure in the squire's coat with the small mouth smiling under the tricky neat mustache, and for once she did not answer as she might have done. Instead she looked down again at her work and for the first time she said to him:

"I would have liked to have had a son."

To be what I'm not and never have been, he thought at once; to do the hard, thrashing, male things I've never done to land or woman or beast; not a son to carry on my blood but hers and Major Husen's, resenting now even her own father's blood in her; the stud, the wooings and the matings, to bear that on, the foalings, the deaths, the cycle turning and returning to the accouplements. He put out his hand and laid it on her shoulder without thinking of the words to use to begin saying it, but simply beginning:

"It's the people we surround ourselves with or get surrounded with, maybe, that seem to make us into something we never would have been. If you'd had a son you wouldn't have had to have been so—so—fearless. That's not quite the word but I mean—"

"I'm not fearless," she said, her head down, her hands working quickly at her knitting.

"Yes, because I'm a coward you had to be fearless," he said. "You found out you had to be fearless a long time ago, too long, and now you don't know how to be afraid any more. But I'm going to be different about things, you've heard me say that before, but this time I'm going to be different. I'm going to try to get into things more, be more active, and make things easier for you. I'd like you to be afraid and come to me afraid, not every day but some days."

"I am afraid," she said, her head down, her eyes on the knitting. For the second that he did not look at her he believed with the same complete perception as before that time did not lapse, in spite of man-conceived divisions

98

neither receded nor advanced, and he heard her voice as his young love's and his young wife's saying:

"I am afraid. I'm afraid for Nan."

✦

The girl worked two hours every night, sometimes longer, with the horse, worked fast with him now that the second week was closing: the half-passage for the first quarter of an hour in the paddock where the cropped grass was resting, and then the turn on the center as the simplest of the three equine turns. "The half-passage," said the textbook she lay reading in the hammock, "consists in making the horse, while keeping his whole body, from nose to croup, parallel with the sides of the enclosure, move sideways, crossing both fore feet and hind feet. The exercise should be performed only when the horse is walking well into his bridle. By asserting a strong pressure of one leg slightly drawn back the horse should move off in the required direction. Both legs on one side should cross the other two (in front, not behind) and he should gain ground all the time. His progression should therefore be at an angle of 45° to the sides of the road or the enclosure."

The second quarter of the hour was the turn on the center, the one turn the horse makes naturally, without instruction: the rider's inner knee the fulcrum, the horse's forehand turning inward, his quarters outward. Not till the last day of the week did she try the circle on two tracks, on the forehand and on the hock, and then "A strong pressure of the inward leg, which should be slightly drawn back, and the hand rein strongly applied," the textbook said. "The horse should make a complete circle, with his head facing the center and the hind legs passing along the circumference." Or for the hock circle, she read in the warm dim drowsy afternoon, with the hammock just moving, not swinging but stirring slightly and nothing more; for this "a strong pressure of the outward leg, in front of the girth, and the outward rein, with the hand on the neck pushing the horse over as it were," and now Candy came across the lawn, walking quickly, silently on rubber soles, dressed in white as if just ready for tennis although he had never so much as thought of tennis in years, but had dressed again, coolly and freshly, to kill an hour of the afternoon. He sat down without a sound, without a word, in the canvas chair by the tin table where the half-empty glass of lemonade was standing and she looked up from her book at him in the moment before he spoke and saw the small shocked face above the polo-shirt's open neck, the color gone from the mouth even. Although he had been well shaven at lunch, or must have been, the skin showed ailing as scalp now through darkish and unexpected bristles.

"Penson," he said, swallowing, and he did not look at her. His bare elbows were braced on the chair's wooden arms and his fingers interlocked before him. She put the book down, closed, and sat up in the hammock, the shape of the net's sag altering as she moved until it took and held her buttocks' shape. "Something's happened to Penson," he said, and his eyes ran from one side to the other, trapped in their sockets like marbles in a pocket. "A horse almost did him in last night. I met his wife in Pellton, ran into her on the street coming from the hospital." His eyes were running fast from the vision of it, and the girl sat before him in the scarcely moving hammock, her bare legs hanging slender and white-skinned out of her skirt and her bare feet, blue-veined and narrow in the unfastened sandals, swinging slightly just above the circle of earth worn under the hammock and the trees where feet had always swung. "Around Buxton, I think she said. He was called in to look at a horse," he went on saying, his eyes running fast, "and the damned farmers didn't hold the animal properly. It was a big draught-horse, heavily shod, and, by God, he got poor Penson square in the face. One point of the heel right in the eye, she said, and the other point hooked the roof of his mouth, and as soon as the brute had him down she says the farm hands ran a mile. They left Penson lying there in the stall calling for help until one or two of them collected their wits and came back and got him out—"

"Bright lads," said the girl, swinging.

"But by that time the horse had trampled his right arm half off, and she says it was Penson who told them what to do. 'Get me to the nearest doctor so he can stop the bleeding,' he told them," and Candy's eyes fled wildly from the sight of it, "but the doctor they got him to took one look and said he wouldn't touch that skull with a yardstick for fear of doing Penson in. 'All right,' said Penson, 'then get me to Pellton Royal Hospital quick as you can,' and she says the doctor drove him the twenty miles in half an hour." Candy's breath was shaking in his mouth but he went on saying: "Penson told the surgeon to give him a local anaesthetic but not to put him out completely because it was an operation he'd always wanted to see done. Trepanning I think they call it, only this time she said the difference was they didn't have to saw out a part of the skull because it had been kicked out already, so all the surgeon had to do was pick out the pieces from the front, and Penson had them put a mirror up where he could see, and there was Penson, Penson, by God, making suggestions!" His tongue came out to run along his lip but it brought no moisture with it, and looking at him from the hammock she thought It's not for Penson he's in a funk like this but for something that might happen to somebody else, perhaps to me or perhaps to himself, something more personal than just fear of theoretic violence but because it's a sample given, not only an instance of what happened to somebody else but of what might happen to him or me sometime, or perhaps just to me. "Three hours on the table," Candy said, "and Penson told the surgeon or the surgeon told Penson, I don't remember which way it was, that the complication could be meningitis. He told him that last night and at four o'clock this morning they recognized the symptoms. He's in for it now," Candy said, the eyes still running from it. "Mrs. Penson says they don't give her any hope. If he comes through, that'll be one more miracle like him having the courage to lie conscious on the operating table telling the surgeon what to do."

"What about the horse?" the girl said. She reached out for the glass of unfinished lemonade and took a swallow of it, but because it was too warm and sour now, she made a face after the first taste, and put it down.

"The horse?" said Candy, for the first time the eyes fixed steadily on her.

"What was wrong with the horse?" she said. "What was Penson called in to look at him for?" She sat swinging slightly in the hammock, the loose, hanging sandals just brushing above the circle worn bare in the grass. "I suppose because of all that stupidity the horse'll go on getting worse, because they'll be afraid to have another vet in to look at him. It wasn't the horse's fault. He was badly managed."

So now the thing is, Candy did not say, his fingers locked together desperately, the thing is we are afraid for you, your mother and I are afraid, we were afraid for you before and now we know exactly: you mustn't go into that blind horse's box any more and groom and feed him. He did not speak but he sat white and shocked before her, his eyes trapped in his face. You'll get Apby or someone else to do it for you, but you can't go in there, you mustn't do it, I forbid you to do it any more. You can't go in there three times a day like that and do all the things you've been doing for him. It's got to stop. Let a man be killed, let a vet die of brain fever, let the entire race of horses stamp out the race of men; but you, my delicate-wristed, my rapt-eyed daughter, you shall stay clear of death by murder, by calculating evil violence, by willful and ruthless vice; you shall remain unstained as the lilies remain pure growing by the water, fragrant as fruit-blossoms, unbruised, unplucked, unsullied. He did not speak but sat before her in his open polo-shirt and his white duck tennis trousers, looking out of his blanched face at her and listening to her.

"She said I could have a fortnight to think it over and now I've thought it over," she was saying, swinging just slightly in the hammock. "Today makes the two weeks and I haven't changed my mind about it, I mean I feel exactly the way I did and I won't let them put Brigand down. I mean, it's not just being stubborn about a thing, but the thing itself isn't the same any more, do you see what I'm trying to say Candy? In a little while I'll be able to show you, but now it's too soon. I have to have more time before I can show you. That's what I want to talk to you about. I want you to tell mother I've got to have more time before I can prove it to her, maybe another fortnight would do. You're on my side, Candy, and you've got to tell mother to give me a little more time."

"More time for what?" he said, the eyes coming helplessly to a halt on her face.

"So I can prove they don't have to destroy him," she said. The hammock swung slightly, rhythmically, imperceptibly as breathing. "If I have more time I can show them what's happened and then they'll see there's no need to destroy him. I can't show you now, I want it to be perfect before I show you." The hammock moved her gently towards him and as gently drew her away. "I'm not glad Penson got hurt," she said, the strange, dream-stupored eyes profoundly and motionlessly drifting. "I'm not glad he got hurt, but if he's in hospital then he couldn't put Brigand down. So I want you to ask her to give me more time, just to allow me ten days longer, just enough—"

"He's got an assistant, Penson," Candy said. "He'll have someone replacing him. You needn't count on that," but he knew exactly what he would do: after a while he would get up from the canvas chair and cross the lawn and begin saying it to his wife, standing beside her wherever she was, his hands in his pockets, offering her half in apology and half in challenge the smile that placated nothing. Whether or not the very words in which he would petition the horse's reprieve were asking as well for an extension of the risks of human death, still he would go to where she fought the recalcitrant roses or whatever other insurgent manifestations of life were being chastised by her hand, and he would ask it, smiling, but still in shame and servility of her. "But, look here, Nancy," he said, staving it off a little longer. "What if you go off again in September? What about that blind horse? What would be the point in keeping him hanging on like that if you weren't here?"

"He'll have his own use by that time, he'll have his own life then," she said, swinging. "You'll see."

He thought suddenly I need a drink, that's what I need, a drink, and he stood up and looked at the watch on his warm arm. Bound to her, he thought, by that, "You're on my side," bound and committed to her, to lie for her, plead, connive. He stood looking down at her bare legs and her bare ankles and the sandals open on the blue-veined insteps' bone, and he thought, What if he kicks you to death out there in the box, what if he does, and he said out loud:

"But I want one thing, Nancy," looking rather wistfully and shyly at her as if on the point of asking some favor for himself instead of merely seeking to spare her from death. "I want you to say you won't go out and groom and feed that horse, Nancy. If I ask your mother to allow him to stay on there another fortnight, you can stay away from his heels, Nancy. You can get Apby to do him down and exercise him up the driveway." He stood in uncertainty and almost in humility before her, wanting the drink and at the same time wanting her obedience to be quickly and submissively given. Just not to be the one to wound her, to thwart her, not ever to evoke the balefulness and the defiance (that's for you, Nan, all for you, he thought of his wife; you can have every drop of her resistance, I don't want any of it for me), not now or ever to see the wide floating eyes focus in exprobration on him. "I'm just saying, Nancy, that I don't want to see your face changed, I don't want you dying in a hospital," he said. "I want you to keep on being and looking the way you are. That Irishman," he said, and he accomplished the little smile, "he mightn't like you either any other way."

She sat below him swinging in the hammock for a while, the face meditative, the foot hanging, and then she said, pronouncing the words slowly so there would be no mistake:

"All right, Candy. That's fair enough. I won't groom Brigand and I won't feed him. From now on I'll let Apby do it. I'll let Apby do him down and feed him and walk him up the drive every day. When I go way my horse'll have to get used to someone else, so he might as well start getting used to it now. I'll let Apby groom him and feed him because you ask me to," she said.

Chapter Six

FIRST Mr. Sheehan wrote about his sister marrying and then his aunt wrote: the Hon. Lady Mary Disalt wrote asking if Nancy Lombe would come up to London as house-guest.

"There you are," said Candy. He looked brightly and saucily over the breakfast table. "They want a double wedding."

"Don't put ideas into her head," said the mother. The tone was light enough but she looked up at the girl with a measuring, a quietly conjecturing eye. "What in the world will you wear? What have you got?" she said to the sport-shirt and the fraying jersey and the too-tight riding breeches. "We'll have to go over to Pellton and get you something decent."

"Why doesn't she wear her spotted leopard with the cream lace insert?" said Candy, and the girl began laughing. She lifted her cup of tea to her mouth as if to hide its wide foolish laughing, but once on her tongue the tea spurted in explosions across the dishes. "Try on her old-gold sheath gown with the dimity bodice," Candy said, and the tea splattered onto the marmalade and the silver cover of the warming dish. "Or her emerald-green smock edged with yellow tulle," he went on saying, and the girl cried out:

"Oh, stop, Candy, stop it! You're so silly!"

"Or her pistache velvet with the raccoon slip?" he said.

"As we used to say at school, 'was it Daniel Boone or the raccoon that gave the knave the name of Boone.'"

"Possum," the girl cried out, her face bright red with laughing. "I'm sure his hat was possum!"

The mother sat reading the Hon. Lady Mary's letter again, breakfast not done yet, and she did not speak, sitting now in that far and elegantly appointed study in which the words had been penned, perhaps on a russet leather-clasped blotting pad and certainly on Chippendale, with the murmur of London penetrating the bottle-bottomed studded panes and the partially drawn velvet hangings, reading: "So we should like to have her come up on Friday night, the seventh of July. Naturally, she will be met at Waterloo and chaperoned to the house." So that gives us ten days, the mother thought, but not the time for anything to be made; and the time is short like that for the very good reason that this highfaluting Mr. James Sheehan couldn't make up his mind until the last moment, not knowing whether he wanted Nancy Lombe to come or whether he didn't until probably yesterday morning. A wedding as presentable as this one is planned and the house party arranged for and invited six weeks ahead, at least six weeks, but it's plain as day that his royal highness decided just in the nick that Nancy was good enough, that Nancy Lombe, the little girl he'd met in Florence at Mrs. Patterson's one afternoon last winter, would make the grade, and would dear Aunt Mary Disalt write to those squirey people down Pellton-way who had this pretty daughter, and it took a bit of persuading because the guest list had been drawn up months ago, but in the end she did. And at least she had the grace to add: "Please excuse the unavoidable tardiness of this, but my

nephew's delayed return from the continent made any planning with him virtually impossible."

"They've given us such short notice, the proper thing
would be to turn them down," the mother said, and she put
the point of toast crowned richly with Danish butter and
bramble-jam into her mouth; but they all knew that the girl
was to go. The mother knew it best perhaps, because knowing that friends, just other people found and called by that
miraculously transforming name, were enough to change a
girl's heart and alter her life for her; knowing this change
might be the overture to final propitiation, the way to muf-
fle at last the sound of horse's hoofs, not any horse's or all
horses' hoofs, but the hoofs of the crazy hunter on his fruit-
less hunt galloping unflaggingly towards death through
their speech and their silence and their struck bargain's
commutation. She began talking of the clothes, shop-bought
they'd have to be, and the sound of the galloping horse
went on, and the mother thought, In London she'll meet
people and she'll see things in their true proportions, but
she'll have to have a suit to travel in, and at least two dresses,
she's outgrown everything, and the horse's hoofs went galloping endlessly and hopelessly towards the unseen goal.
Without pronouncing the name to herself even, the mother
decided, It has to be done one day and it can be done without a scene, tears, arguments, if she's out of the house, and
then when she comes home she'll have the fact to face, the
absolutely done and finished thing. "Three dresses, you'll
have to have three," she said to her daughter's bright red
convulsed face. Candy was swaying in the arms of the
dance, his checked coat humped up across his neck and

shoulders as he waltzed between the breakfast table and the sideboard, his eyes half-closed, his head back, singing:

" 'Don't tell my mother I breakfast on gin, Don't let the old folks know. Don't tell my father I'm living in sin, He'd never survive the blo-ow-ow-ow!' "

"For heaven's sake, stop singing that vile song before the servants hear you," the mother said, conjecturing the dresses, three complete outfits it would have to be, a new suit for traveling and two dresses to wear in the city. Candy started jigging, his hands on his hips, across the varnished dining-room floor.

" 'I'm one of the ruins Cromwell knocked abaht a bit,' " he sang. " 'Just *one* of the ruins Cromwell knocked abaht a bit,' " his feet nimbly, quickly, pattering time. " 'Blimey, there reely isn't a doubt of it, All the 'istory books they shout of it—' "

"Is it you who's going up to London to the house party or is it Nancy?" the mother said, and looking at him she began to laugh. But the girl had ceased laughing now. She held her hands down in her lap, watching languidly, drowsily something outside the window perhaps, or perhaps only hearing the same quick, clapping passage of the hunter's feet on road or cobbles or muffled and throbbing across turf. She said:

"I'll go up for the day only. I'll go just for the wedding. I won't stay three days away."

So the argument that never found conclusion began groping anew past the minutiae of this issue as past the others and beyond it to the declaration of probity itself: the mother's voice strained thin with bitterness and hopelessness and, at last, with fury, across the breakfast table and later across the lunch table, before it turned back from the stubborn, outlandish but insoluble pledge the girl had made to some equivocal young honor, to some unperjured but infuriating loyalty. So there it was left, none of the spirit solved nor the will yet broken to will, but in abeyance: the girl would go up on the Friday afternoon and spend the night there, only one night away, and be down on the afternoon train that brought her in just before tea time Saturday. After the first moment of wondering, she knew there was nothing to fear; and now that the mother's voice returned to hopelessness, planning the suit and the one dress instead of the two, the girl lying in the hammock counted the granted days that had not yet elapsed, thinking I can go because I have until Monday and because Apby can feed and water him and perhaps exercise him, perhaps even that. She would go too because of this: because she could see Mr. Sheehan clearly only in profile, sitting beside her on the sofa at Mrs. Patterson's in Florence and leaning forward to lift up the plate of sandwiches and pass it, but the rest of his face had perished; the remembered hairless young hand out of the brown tweed jacket's sleeve, the locks of crinkly, rather difficult hair worn too long for convention, and the lobeless, narrow ear with the hair waving thick above it, light brown, or perhaps only touched with light in places, or perhaps burned light by the Italian sun, had not expired but she could not meet his eyes. Below the concave temple's level were the deep tiny lines (just under the eyebrow's dark delicate extremity), worn there by too much dry chortling at wit (his own or anybody else's) or else from squinting hard against the weather, radiating finely from the eye's tip. But whenever he turned in memory to pass the plate of sandwiches, the vision failed: the mouth, the nose, the eyes went out and only the brow remained with the long wrinkles across it like the marks of tide left on a beach, and the widow's peak giving a heart's shape to the face. Now that he had written her, and the aunt had written, he did not cease leaning in profile, only in profile, over the textbook's page, the hairless, youthful hand following the line as she read it:

"The 'approach' is the three strides the horse makes immediately before taking off. The problem is to get the horse to jump off his hocks, at a suitable distance away from the fence, and to jump completely under the rider's control. The rider must decide in good time upon the last three strides, counting 'one-two-three-up,' and regulate his horse's pace accordingly." She who had ridden and jumped since before she was five now making a study of it and reading: "Keep the horse at a controlled canter up to thirty feet from the fence. The length of a stride in a controlled canter is about six feet. At thirty feet from the fence increase this stride to seven feet, then to eight, and finally to nine. At this point you are six feet from the jump and should then give the horse the office for the leap—" and Mr. Sheehan leaned across the page in profile, the side of his mouth laughing, his eye squeezed up with laughing and the thick dark lashes thrusting forward, and the girl stretched in the librating, the almost imperceptibly moving hammock thought, I don't know whether I like him or not, I don't know if I really like him.

And now the rains returned again, starting in one afternoon as she lay reading the book and swinging slightly, the bare sandaled foot hanging near the ground. First the clouds gathered up behind the house and then the sun went, half the visible world lying in yellow murk for a space and half in blue rich foreboding, and then the first single shafts of rain came down, slanting long and silvery past the foliage, falling at intervals beyond her haven like deliberately lanced spears. Then came the true hard rain, driving down the lawn all afternoon and streaming along the window panes at supper; after the first quick stabs of lightning and the thunder had passed, the rain continued swiftly and relentlessly falling across the country, setting its quiet, dreary pace in the evening and then buckling down to it for the night. When the girl awoke at one in the morning, it was still raining quietly outside. She had brought her mackintosh up in the evening from below and laid it over the chair with her riding breeches, and now she put it on and tied the rubber handkerchief over her hair before going out the window. She thought I might have remembered my Wellingtons, sliding in her breeches and plaid wool bedroom slippers down the spouting drainpipe, but she had forgotten them the night before and forgot them now by the time she reached the stable. She was thinking, I just want him to be there, waiting inside, that's all I ask. I don't care if I'm soaked to the skin if he'll just understand and be there. And once inside the stable she saw him leaning beyond the shaded lantern he had set by the stall: Apby with his own black mackintosh shining with rain as he saddled the hunter.

"So you did come!" she said, and he looked up and touched his cap's beak, saying: "You said to be here, Miss," and leaned to the girth-straps again.

"I thought maybe when you saw it was raining," she said, and as she pushed in sideways past the horse's tail and croup and past the leaning groom, the blind horse turned his head on his shoulder towards the sound of her voice and her approach. She stood by his head, running her wet hand under his forelock, and she said: "I'm going up to London tomorrow. That's why I wanted to see you tonight. I wanted to ask you to carry on without me for the night and day I'm up in the city. I mean, I want you to put Brigand through his work-out the way I've been doing. One to half-past two, say, tomorrow night, and then when I come back I'm going to show them."

"Yes, Miss," said the groom, still leaning, not lifting his head.

"You can keep him on the figure eight with change and the half-passage at the canter," she said. She drew her hand down the short rough hair on the nasal bone. "You can try him out tonight with me on the half-passage and change, and if you can keep him going while I'm away, that'll be saving—" She thought of saying "my life" and then, because this brought it so near to "his life," she suddenly crossed her fingers against bad luck and stopped speaking. As Apby straightened up her eyes slid towards him a little cautiously, in slow, tentative induction. "Look," she said. "Another reason I wanted to see you tonight. I want to make him jump." She watched the groom sideways down the stall, her hand moving under the horse's forelock. "I want to take him over a fence tonight," she said.

The groom stood in his brightly gleaming coat, part in the lantern's light and part in the stable's dark, his cap on and its shadow cast grotesquely to the ceiling's beams, his hands on his hips, his dwarfed legs bowed, facsimile in miniature of tough and indomitable and muscular man.

"You can't do it, Miss," he said. "You can't make a blind horse jump. You can't do more than what nature allows for. You're just fixing him for a broken shoulder or broken neck—"

"I set up a knife-rest in the paddock three nights ago," she said, not paying any heed but standing there half-smiling, bringing her hand slowly down the pan of the hunter's cheek. "He took it. He took it back and forth a dozen times. When I come back I'll stretch him out on broader jumps."

"You can't do it," said Apby. He stood there on the straw bedding, his hands knuckled on his hips and the light shining through the arch and bow of his legs in their leather gaiters. He had shoved the beak of his cloth cap up and now it stood erect from the lining's edge above his creased short brow. "You've done up to now with a crock as what I've never heard of no one else doing, but you nor nobody can't give him the sight the time he needs it quick like that for gauging width and height. You can't do it," he said, and he said it again as he extinguished the lantern and then followed her and the horse out over the beam and into the steadily raining night. "You can't do it," he said, closing the stable door and buttoning his mackintosh's collar up to his chin while she mounted quickly from the ground. "You can't say to any horse, living or dead, this is so high this time and the next time it's so high so get ready for it, not unless he's got the power to see. Not unless you had just one jump fixed for him, say knee-high, and took him over it twenty times running, and even then. Even then," he said, "you couldn't do it."

"What I said to you first about why I wanted you to come out here tonight," she said, turning back to him on the saddle, "that wasn't the whole thing. I could have said that to you tomorrow morning or yesterday afternoon just as well. What I really wanted was for you to be here for the jump. I want you to stand at the thirty-foot mark in the paddock and call out one, two, three at the moment I cross it so I'll know how far it is to the fence."

"You can't do it," Apby said, following the horse's footfalls in the rain, not going up the stud-farm road tonight but the long way around by the running water to the paddocks. "You can't have a horse's eyes go and not pay for it, some way you got to pay for it. There wouldn't be no justice anywheres if a blind horse could do it as good as a horse without a flaw or a failing. You can't do what's impossible, because if you could there wouldn't be no end—" and not hearing the uneasy and exasperated words but only the sound of his complaint, the girl turned in the saddle and went on talking over her shoulder to him in the steadily falling rain.

"That'll tell me and tell him, that'll tell us both when we've got to the approach," she said, "and then I'll know when to give him the rise and take him over. You'll stand at the thirty-foot mark where I laid it out this morning, no, yesterday morning by this time, and you'll call out one, two, three. . . ."

"And to think," the groom's voice went on as he came booted and clopping behind, "it was me that begun this, started you off that night in the paddocks when you had him out with me— If I was to do the right thing by everybody, you and the horse included, what I'd do now is tell Mrs. Lombe what's going on, get 'er up out-a-wer bed no matter if it's middle of the night or tomorrow morning, and she'd put 'er foot down and seen it was put a stop to. If I was to do what I ought to be doing now instead of—" He took one hand out of his mackintosh pocket and wiped the rain down his cheeks the way a comedian pretends to wipe the smile from his face, and then he started running clumsily forward through the mud and rain, stumbling ahead until he got to the horse's evenly and rhythmically riding croup and passed it, and then kept abreast the stirrup with the girl's plaid wool bedroom slipper thrust soaking in it while he said: "If I was to go to the house now and tell Mrs. Lombe, she wouldn't stand for it. She'd put a stop to it all right before anything worse came to happen, jumping on a stone-blind horse the way you say on a night that even frogs would stay home in. If I was to go back to the house now and get—" .

"Only you wouldn't," the girl said, riding straight ahead. "You wouldn't do it because I need you to stand at the thirty-foot mark. If you didn't stand there, then something might happen because I couldn't judge close enough when to give him the rise. I worked it out from the book that maybe he'll jump this way if he won't jump any other. I wouldn't ask it for any other horse but just give him his rein and let him take off when he liked, maybe not elegant, according to the book, but that's the way I've always done it. The book says—"

"Oh, the book!" said Apby. Either she halted the horse or he halted of himself, but her voice and his movement ceased at the same instant and the groom looked up and, understanding what it was now, went ahead to open the paddock gate. She heard the hinges cry out and, waiting, heard Apby beginning the same arguments over in the same vexed, grieved tone.

"You can't do it no more than anybody could do it, a trainer couldn't do it and no book can tell you how to take a blind, dumb, unwitting, unwilling beast—" and she leaned forward and patted the horse's shoulder on which the rain poured like sweat.

"So you wouldn't let me down," she said as she rode in past Apby. "You'll stand at the thirty-foot mark where I made it this morning. I'll show it to you."

"Anyways," Apby said, letting the gate swing back, "if he breaks his back at it that'll be all right. They'll have to put him down tomorrow then, Mr. Penson or no Mr. Penson."

"Stand here, Apby," she said, bringing the horse to a halt in the grass. "Stand here. You can feel the bricks making a cross. That's it."

"You can't do it," Apby said again, and out of the little distance she had ridden away already, she said:

"I have done it. I did it alone with him over the knife-rest when there was moonlight, ten, fifteen times back and forth. The only difference is neither of us can see tonight. You stay where you are." The rain came quickly, quietly down, not in voluble articulation as on a house's roof or windows, but striking the face, the naked hands in silence, dropping steadily, as if forever, on the head and shoulders, the bent legs, beating softly as a moth's wings in the trees, until it was rain no longer after a while but the accumulated presence of water, more salient than the dark's or any human presence, like the presence of a vast and swiftly flowing, unseen river passing within arm's reach through the night. Apby stood with water trickling from his cap's stuff down across his face, water dripping unceasingly from the now lowered beak, one drop following another in rivulation to the corners of his mouth, into his ears until, like a bather, he put his forefingers into the ears' orifices and wrung them. "Damn the rain," was the last thing he heard her say before he heard the horse coming, and then a little later, either in imagination or in reality, saw coming towards him the dim cantering shape.

"She might have picked any other night to do it," he said half aloud, as if speaking to someone standing there with him for comfort's sake or else to split the blame with. He ran the back of his hand along his upper lip, under his water-beaded nose, and shook the drops off, and now the splatter of the horse's feet, the wind and thrash of his coming was almost ready to pass. He felt the movement of the air, the breath, the throb, heard even the saddle's creaking leather and the tossed bit's jangle, as if someone had opened a window or pushed open a door near him to let in these sounds he had not heard before in a vast darkened and silenced hall; and as the thing rushed past he leapt back and called the words out. "One, two, three!" he called out like a man crying desperately out from shore into the hopeless dark and wind to the floundered and drowning lost in a storm-pounded sea.

Mr. Sheehan, she thought for an instant, said that time in Florence that nobody should start riding too young, children being either too bold or too timid or both at the same time, and then the bold ones crack up going fast and they've no nerve left to go on the rest of their lives with, and the timid ones go on being shy with horses, or danger, or other people, or with themselves; their spirits, not their bodies, crippled. Mr. Sheehan said, England, the horse-growing country and the country as well of all the misfits, the hug-ger-muggers, the reticent, the mum, the evaders, because why, because what? because what except stuck up on a horse's back since generations and licked from the get-away, the lip set, both upper and lower, the eyes taught not to quail, and the heart broken in two by funk or daring at the age of five or younger. Take away the horses and you would have a fine upstanding race of men, the Britons, said Mr. Sheehan, the side of his face in profile squinted up either against laughing or against the drifting Irish weather, and for an instant she remembered the first time being thrown: the hack had cantered her up the lane to the top of the hill and there he had reared for no reason except "frightened by the bush because the bush unexpectedly turned and waved a branch," without warning dropping her the long way down. I remember being sick, terrifically sick, she thought, perhaps passing Apby at the thitry-foot mark now, and mother made me mount quickly again as soon as I was finished being sick. "If you don't mount right away," mother said, "you'll start crying and then you won't want to get up on a horse again," and now Apby's voice called out, "One, two, three," and she put her teeth together and thought in sudden wild jubilation, Tomorrow I'll be able to tell Mr. Sheehan that at thirty feet from the fence I increased the stride to seven feet, then to eight, and finally to nine, at this point being, as near as I could judge in the dark, six feet from the jump and I gave my horse the office for the leap.

"Bat," she said quickly. "I can't see any more than you

can but we're going to take it." She let the head free then and the loins free, and her weight moved swiftly into the knees as they clasped the saddle-flaps. The balls of the feet were riding lightly in the stirrup irons now and she held him firmly to the fence with her legs. At once she felt him rising strongly but sweetly under her, the mouth limber, the neck pliant even though stretched to go, no sense of heat or excitement confusing him but the blood as temperate as if he still cantered easily across the paddock. Just as they cleared what, from conjecture, must have been the rail though lost and undelineated in the night's and the falling water's obscurity, she thought of the other side and the wet grass where he might bog or slip at the landing, and she said again: "Damn it, oh, damn the rain."

She leaned with him, the body that had followed through the rise and the soaring now bending with him through the descent, and as his forefeet struck the ground her knees and ankles caught the shock and broke it but her hands did not move on the reins. She let him stride on for twenty yards or more before she pulled him up and turned him on his hocks, and halted there in the rain and darkness and listening to the coming and going of his breath, she called out to the groom:

"Apby, I say, Apby, come and open the gate for us," her own voice sounding ringing and clear. "Apby!" she called, like someone tipsy with triumph, drunk and reeling with it. "Apby, hurry up! I want to take him over again."

Chapter Seven

ON FRIDAY afternoon, just after lunch time, the girl went up to London in her new suit, carrying her little overnight bag in her hand, and nothing happened in the country until the Saturday morning. It was then, standing by the sitting-room window and looking into the flowered and damp emptiness of still another day, that Candy saw them emerge from somewhere, perhaps from the main road outside where a two-seated car might now be standing halted close to the bank: the back of a man he had not seen before in khaki riding-breeches and a sport-shirt, and his wife in dark blue spotted all over its broad skirt and blouse with white, and her summer hat on, the sailor hat which came out of some undivulged hiding place each end of May or in the early days of June, depending on the weather. He watched them descend the drive, making the gestures of talk, and pass the rock garden where the purple foxgloves stood nobly if a little shabbily flowering in the moist sunlight, and pass the wayfaring-tree at the curve and go from sight. For a moment, standing at the window, he wondered and then without any feeling of surprise, he knew. He knew it exactly, as if the words had been said to him and knew now, moreover, that it was for this the quiet and lull of the day before and the night had been preparing. Through some irremediable error the sun had come out that morning, but otherwise the unmistakable stage was set.

When they had gone from sight he walked into the dining room and although it was only just gone ten he took the decanter of whiskey out. The ordinary glasses were kept in the pantry, and sadly, quietly he thought, I cannot go out and get one any more than I can go out there and go into the stable and stop them doing it. He opened the sideboard door, stooping to it, and selected one of the small embossed porter glasses and set it on the table, and then he filled it three-quarters full with whiskey and set the decanter down, fitting the glass stopper to it, and he drank the whiskey off at once. He thought, They'll do it humanely, they're bound to do it humanely, and he looked almost peacefully at the bottom of the empty glass. If I had any arguments or any reasons to give them I could go out there, or if I could walk into the stable like a man with a wallet fat in his pocket and slap the sides of it and say, This happens to be, just happens to be my horse, not yours, my lady. He was bought by me, paid for by me, purchased under the rules of warranty (only I never got the certificate because I had two drinks instead), as sound in wind and eyes, quiet to ride, has been hunted and capable of being hunted, so pack up your chalk and your pistol and your vet, whoever he is, in your old kit bag and go back to gardening. They'll do it humanely, he thought, and the feeling of peace spread marvelously through him, something better than mere respite or truce but the final, absolute conciliation through performed and indisputable act. The responsibility is being taken off my shoulders, he thought gently, forbearingly, the issue is being removed from my hands. I have no authority, no jurisdiction, even if I moved now towards the door and out it I could not save that horse, and the sense of actionless, speechless bliss rose richly in him; I am powerless, helpless because they know their business and I have none yet, I never found it; my wife will see that the target is properly indicated and the man in breeches will make use of the humane killer to the conclusion of this drama, this minor but grotesquely aggrandized tragedy which will fade slowly but unerringly into the past. It is not disaster but the one logical solution, he thought, and the voice drifted from some far dim plane of memory to hearing now, repeating as it had years back repeated all day at fifteen-minute intervals across the air, "The King's life is drawing peacefully to a close."

After the second porter-glassful was drunk, Candy put his hand to his back pocket and took his silver and leather hip-flask out. He unscrewed the cap and drew the cork out with his teeth, tipping his head on the side to do it, and then he filled it up from the decanter. He did not spill any, but because a little spread wet at the top, he ran his tongue around the screw-cap's thread, then corked the flask and twisted the top back on and slipped it under his jacket again. Or stamp down there, he thought, and take no nonsense from them, the artist out of pocket, out of luck, but painting alone, accomplishing alone experiments in style, subject, and treatment, working alone and making a name that people listen for in city exhibitions and museums, look for in catalogues and magazines, so that even a wife or even a vet's assistant would listen. He looked at the decanter in dispassionate meditation a moment and then he filled the porter glass again. Penson drawing his last breaths, it may be, while I stand here drinking, kicked towards kingdom come and landing on the threshold, and yet I'd face my

Maker saying they haven't a damned bit of evidence against that blind staggerer out there in the stable, not a shred of anything except that he can't see the day ahead to face the firing squad. You've got to die, he said suddenly, putting the glass down. Horse, it's your turn to die. This time it's not Penson or me but you, horse not man, you blank-eyed espial spying upon the secrets of eternity, you milky-eyed deserter. You're no good to anyone, he said, but he was looking at his own face in the sideboard mirror. Because this was the affair culminated at last between himself and the very fiber and substance of his going on, he did not begin thinking of Nancy until after the fifth glass of whiskey; and when he thought of her he put the glass stopper for the last time into the decanter and went at once, walking carefully but without any semblance of drunkenness, upstairs to his own bedroom and pulled open the bottom drawer of the dresser. From under the neatly folded cardigans, he took out the revolver and made sure that it was loaded, and then he put it into his jacket pocket. There were two more glasses of liquid left in the decanter and he drank them fast.

"That makes everything neat and tidy," he said, but when he stooped to retrieve the glass stopper which had dropped to the ground, his head spun slowly, so he helped himself erect again by holding to the table with one hand. Then he started walking, careful and trim in his squire's jacket, his silk kerchief folded on his neck, down the faintly steaming drive.

The sliding door was standing open beyond the wayfaring-tree and Mrs. Lombe and the young man in breeches were in the stable. They were not in the hunter's stall but talking together as they stood on the timber floor, and beyond the box's gate the hunter's quarters shone in the light. At the first sound of Candy's step on the wood, his wife turned her head with her sailor hat on it and said:

"This is Mr. Lombe, Mr. Harrison. I've had Mr. Harrison over this morning while Nan's up in London to do what has to be done."

Candy stood against the daylight in the door, a rather jaunty figure with his hands in his jacket pockets, the back of the wrist and the left thumb showing, but this time the right thumb was out of sight. He nodded his head either in greeting or dismissal and teetered upwards, his legs planted wide apart, on his clean crepe soles.

"Where's Apby?" he said. "Does Apby know what's going on?"

"I sent him off early." She smiled a quick, tolerant, although impatient-seeming smile. "He's having the day off in Pellton. I told him I'd see the hunter got his midday meal. I haven't said anything to anybody. I just want to get it done as quickly and quietly as possible. It's not a pleasant job of work for anyone concerned. I had Richards take the mare to the village to have her shod."

"So there wouldn't be any witnesses, not so much as a mare looking on, what?" said Candy, and now her eye on him altered as she began to suspect it. "Where do you intend to do it?" Candy said. Since that first step over the threshold he had not moved and his eyes had not shifted from her face, so if he had been asked then he could not have said whether the man called Harrison was short or tall, or what the color of his hair or what his age was, only that he remembered the khaki breeches and the gaiters walking down the drive. "Where is justice to be meted out?" he said loudly, sardonically.

"Mr. Harrison is the huntsman from the local hunt," Mrs. Lombe said, saying the words pleasantly and exactly to him, as if it were a child's small, stubborn figure, not a man's and not her husband's, who stood teetering against the light. "He's been kind enough to offer to do it for us. He's an expert at it. I've arranged for the haulers to come at eleven and take the body away."

"Which body?" said Candy, and now as good as if his breath had been wafted to her over the smell of clean horse and fresh bedding and clean mixture in the stable, she knew the bitter and unacceptable truth: that he was drunk, drunk at ten in the morning, that it was not curiosity that held him standing there haranguing but drunken opposition; not only drunk but drunk before lunch for a change and drunk before a stranger.

"Don't be an idiot, Candy," she said, laughing quickly, nervously, and glancing at Mr. Harrison in invitation to him to do the only possible thing and laugh. "You'd better go back to the house so Mr. Harrison can get on with it."

But Candy began crossing the stable now, walking blank-eyed, blank-faced, deliberately toward them, not swaying or deviating from the invisible line his intention had drawn, but walking carefully and deliberately at them as if they were no longer there now that he had started walking directly to where he wanted to go. They did not obstruct his way, but as he came they drew apart, each of them drawing to one side as a crowd might have drawn apart to allow the passage of a vehicle that ran on tracks and could not alter its course, and Candy passed between the two people who stared, the man in curiosity and the woman in wonder at him, and walked to the stall where the horse stood, its head hanging peacefully now across the gate. Candy took his left hand from his pocket and put it on the latch, and the horse threw his head up and Candy hesitated an instant, and then turned his head too and looked back at the two people standing, in their turn outlined and faceless, against the sunlight in the open stable-door.

"I just wanted to know," he said, almost imperceptibly swaying. "I just wanted to ask you before I go in there how Mr. Penson is, Mr. Har— I'd like to know."

The young man took a step or two towards him—young, thought Candy, seeing him for the first time now as he stood in relief against the yellowish brightness of the day outside, young only because the legs tapered in the breeches and the shoulders were broad and unsloping, for he could not see the features of the face or the color of the hair.

"I was just telling Mrs. Lombe," the man said in a strangely gentle, girl-like voice. "I was just telling her he died. He died last night."

"So an eye for an eye, a horse for a man, that's the way you look at it," said Candy, sardonically, but the whiskey was swinging hard and sickening in his head now and he held to the gate's wood for support. "A life for a life is what you think—" He saw Mrs. Lombe with the old sailor hat on coming towards him and he remembered I mustn't take my right hand out of my pocket until I'm ready. I can get the gate open with my left hand, like this, and now he had come through it and he stood on the oaten straw bedding by the horse now, and the gate was closed between him and his wife and the man she called Mr. Harrison.

"He's so expert," he said, holding to the wood and pressing away from the horse's shoulder in the stall, "that he could probably do it without drawing the chalkline or do it with his eyes closed only he's not going to. The minute he takes out his revolver, I take out mine."

"Candy, come out," said Mrs. Lombe, but the conviction had lapsed from her voice. Candy was standing as far from the horse as he could get, the bordeaux-red silk kerchief around his throat because he hadn't shaved yet, the small of his back against the rough wood of the stall. "Please be reasonable, please come out," she said, but the power had gone from her. She stood with the straw hat pushed up off her forehead, seeking to say it with dignity.

"I'll come out when Nancy gets back," he said. "My little girl will come out here and she'll understand what I'm trying to do. She'll take shifts here with me, all summer if it has to be, hunger-strike, sleep-strike, drink-strike," he said, and at the last words the feeling of tears welled in him; and oh, heavens, heavens, thought the woman standing on the other side of the gate, what have I done that I should have to stand here before a stranger and hear him turning maudlin? What have I done that it should have to happen like this? Oh, spare me, spare me. "And if you try to stop Nancy's marriage it'll be the same thing. I won't have you interfering with her and stopping her whatever she wants to do, lift a finger, go to a dance, have a horse of her own like—" And ah, unjust, unjust, thought the mother bitterly. Who was it picked out the clothes for her to go up to London, who was it had found the school for her in Florence last year? But there had been so many years of it now that it was for nothing else but the stranger's presence that she

cared. "I'll wait here for my little girl," Candy went on saying in the same low-pitched and vagrant and scarcely de-
fiant voice, "and you can't do anything to me because this
time I've got the upper hand, for once I've got it. You've
got the money but this time I tricked you, I fooled you,
you can't field marshal me out of here, you can't major-
domo me, you can't even bribe me—" Oh, sordid, sordid,
thought the mother in grief as she looked at the small con-
torted flushed face, ageless and queer as a dwarf's, turning
from one side to the other in fear of death and fear of life
on the other side of the gate. In a moment she looked towards Mr. Harrison and whether the actual word was said
or merely indicated, they both moved in simultaneous dignity and forbearance towards the door, crossing the timber
to the threshold, and there the young man stood differen-
tially to one side to let her pass before him out into the
light. "You can go, but it won't make any difference to
me," Candy called out, but then as the blind horse shifted
a little nervously on the straw, he lowered his voice. "That's
all right," he said, but when he looked at the massive shoulder and the strong hanging head his blood swooned in him.
He stood leaning against the side of the stall, his hands in
his pockets, seeking not to see the great, living, breathing
beast with its eyes clogged blue and milky beneath the
long, luxuriant lash, and then he took his left hand from the
jacket's pocket and felt out the flask, and braced it against
his ribs with his palm, the left hand's fingers fumbling off
the cap. He did not stir his right hand but drew the cork
out with his teeth and drank, and while he drank the horse
brought his lowered head across the straw, the wide, soft
nostrils seeking quiveringly for cognizance until the nose

reached the shoes' tips and lipped across them, the monstrous, vacuous, ingesting suction of a snail mounting the ankles and the trousers to the jacket, and when the man brought his arm carefully down and his hand with the flask in it he dared move no longer but stood flattened against the stall's wood, waiting, the flask extended in his stricken hand. The horse's head lifted slowly, searchingly, the ears back, the hairs in the nostrils trembling in the blasts of breath, and now that the lips came blindly fumbling across his shoulder to his face, the cry of terror ripped from Candy's throat. "For Christ's sake!" he screamed, and the horse flung his head away in fright, swinging in the box until his quarters stood trembling now before the man, the long black tail twitching across his buttocks and the points of his hocks. "I can't, I can't," Candy said under his breath and he began whimpering as he leaned against the boards. "I'm afraid, I have a right to be afraid," he said, but now that the horse had ceased to move he managed to cork the flask, his left hand shaking, and slip it into his back pocket. Then he stood quiet there better than a quarter of an hour, his hands out of sight in his pockets, the dream of dauntlessness and sedulity vaguely augmenting and as vaguely waning, and at the last instant of fading reversing to a stronger, clearer, dizzier amplification. At the end of that little while, Mrs. Lombe and the huntsman came through the door and crossed the stable again.

"Mr. Harrison and I have been talking things over," she began in the measured, pleasant voice that must bring concurrence to logic in its wake. "Mr. Harrirson thinks it might be very dangerous for you to stay in there with that horse. I explained to him the horse was not accustomed to being handled by you and he says that's where the great danger lies. It's strangers that worry them when there's anything wrong." He stood with the small of his back held against the boards, his eyes fixed sightless on the horse's rump and the long black tail that swept at intervals across it, and he did not speak. "If you're making this absurd scene for Nancy's sake," she went on, "I assure you she'd rather come home to find her ailing horse dead than to find her father in hospital—"

"Mr. Lombe," said the huntsman in his girl-like wounded voice, "it's scarcely taking the long view of things to—"

It was not Candy's passive opposition now that stopped them both, but without any warning he began to sing, lifting his head so that the back of it rested against the stall's boards, and his throat came free of the silk kerchief as he sang loudlessly, tunelessly what words he remembered of what remnants of song he salvaged from the cahotage of terror and drink and despair.

" 'I saw England's king from the top of a bus, He was riding in state so he didn't see us,' " he sang, bawling it out, and the horse flicked his ears. " 'And though—oh, tra, tra, tra, te-de-dum—oh, by the Saxons we once were oppressed, I cheered, God forgive me, oh, God, oh, God, forgive me, I cheered with the rest, I—' "

Mrs. Lombe stepped a little nearer and spoke his name, and he glanced quickly at her and began at once:

" 'I'm one of the ruins Cromwell knocked abaht a bit, I'm *one* of the ruins Cromwell knocked abaht a bit, oh, tra, la, la, la! Outside the Cromwell Arms last Saturday night I was one of the—' "

When the haulers came a little after eleven, Mrs. Lombe

went to the door with dignity and sent them off, offering to pay them extra if they would be kind enough to come back in the afternoon. Candy had been singing: " 'You remember young Peter O'Loughlin, of course? Well, here he is now at the head of the force! I met him one day while crossing the Strand—oh, God, oh, God bless him, he held up the street with one wave of his hand,' " but when he heard the men speaking outside and saw her go, proudly and discreetly as a lady might, to give them their directions, he turned his head towards the open door and shouted: " 'Don't tell my mother I'm living in sin, Don't let the old folks—' " and they closed the door and left him to it. All through lunch time he stood motionless in the stall with the small of his back against the boards, and at two he had finished the whiskey. The horse had dropped his head and began eating his bedding for they had not watered or fed him since the morning meal. It was almost three o'clock when the haulers came back: he heard their horses and their voices outside in the sunlight, and then Mr. Harrison opened the stable door and he and Mrs. Lombe crossed the timber briskly together. At a little distance from the box they came to a stop.

"You must be very hungry," she said, standing there slightly in advance of the huntsman. "I had them put out some roastbeef sandwiches and beer on the veranda for you, so if you'll just come along—"

"No," said Candy, looking at the horse. "No, it's all right. You can't trick me." He was talking thick now, leaning against the side of the stall. "I'm waiting here for my little girl, I'm waiting, I'm on the side of civilization. This horse, he isn't a horse any moren any of us are horses, he's the forces of good against the forces of destruction, he's me, just as much me as artist, foreigner, just as much an outcast, he's freak and he's love, he's got something to do with love as it works out against—against this, this empire building and this susspression of the native, what you said the other night about Gandhi being so ugly himself, thin and his teeth out and his gums like that the way you would talk about a horse, you said he was such a freak you didn't care what his beliefs were and didn't think he could have any looking like—well, this horse is against that sort of thing. He's for love. All right," he said, "now we've got it straight. This horse, he's all wrong and wherebyfore he's against everything that is your right and the world's right and Mr. Har— He's me by this time, and he's Nancy I think, or he's me and Nancy getting off to another country where everybody who speaks English is a foreigner, not only me. He's my horse, if he's a horse any more, and I bought him with your money, yes, all right, all rr-r-r-right, your money, but I bought something else at the same time, making the same purchase, my dear, something you haven't seen yet but it's there keeping me in the stable and in the stall until you get out of it and there doesn't have to be any explanation for him," mumbling it, half-crying it as he stood with his hands in his pockets staring at the horse's rump.

Mrs. Lombe made the imperceptible sign to the huntsman or spoke the unheard word, and immediately he stepped forward.

"Mr. Lombe," he said in his winning, girl-like voice, "won't you come out with us now and let events take their course?"

Candy turned his head and looked at them, perhaps assuring himself that he had heard it right, and then he began to laugh. With the small of his back pressed in against the stall's boards he began shaking with silent grotesque laughter.

"Let events *what?*" he wheezed through his laughing. "Let them do what?" He leaned his shoulders back now, his mouth half open, growing sick with laughter. "Let events—"

Mrs. Lombe again made the immediately understood sign to the young man, and again he began speaking.

"Mr. Lombe," he said, "we don't want to do it at all but if you don't come out we shall have to ask the hauler's men outside to help us. This horse has been condemned by two leading veterinary-surgeons, one of them dead now, killed in the act of discharging his duty—" and Candy's fit of strangling laughter cut off the sound of the huntsman's voice and the color came up his girlish throat and spread across his jaws. "Killed," he went on after a moment, with his eyes dropped now, "because he stood behind a horse the way you're standing now, Mr. Lombe, in the stall of an ailing, unpredictable animal," and Candy lay weak with laughing against the boards. "I said he was killed in the discharge of his duty," said the huntsman, his high voice trembling as he raised it to be heard. "While you, Mr. Lombe, are obstructing mine and wasting my Saturday for me—" and Candy's hilarious gasps rose now to cries of laughter and then stopped short in incredulous amazement.

"*Your* Satur— Mr. Har—? Your—?" he began, and the laughter convulsed him again. "Oh, please, pull-ease, stop being funny! Oh, pll-ease, pll-ease, Mr. Har—" He threw back his smooth neat little head again and the laughter squeezed out of his eyes and out of the strange contortion of his mouth. "For Christ's sake, pll-ease!" he said, and Mrs. Lombe turned and walked to the stable door and opened it. When she came back the hauler's men were with her, three good, stout countrymen who came through the door after her and stood waiting, ill-at-ease, beside her.

"Will you be so kind," she said quietly to them, but her spirit was bowed in grief and humility in her: so it has come to this, it has come to this. "Will you be good enough to assist the gentleman outside so that he will be out of danger," she said.

The three men stood awkwardly there a moment, their arms bare in their short-sleeved collarless shirts, their shoes good and almost stylish-looking as the shoes of Devonshire workmen are likely to be. They looked uncertainly at one another, and at Mrs. Lombe in her sailor hat, awkwardly seeking, and in too much of a dilemma to feign any other emotion, the unmistakable side of respectability. And then the huntsman made the gesture before them: standing with his face and his right arm averted from Candy's sight in case Candy had turned his head to see, he lifted his hand as if it held a glass in it, raised it to drink, once, twice, and then a third time. His mouth shaped the one word but he did not say it to them: drunk. Here was the shared joke now, the inaudibly communicated truth, and once in on it with the gentry the three hauler's men smiled, neither broadly nor sheepishly but simply in recognition, and after looking once more at one another for confirmation, they took the thing on. First Mrs. Lombe stepped forward, the huntsman walking to one side of her and a little back, perhaps out of native and habitual precaution, and close behind them followed the hauler's men. For an instant Candy did not see them as the march across the boards began but stood leaning back against the wood, his eyes fixed on the horse's motionless rump as if subduing and mastering it by sight alone. He leaned against the stall's side, his hands clenched in his pockets, having entered now another and more violent plane of fear. If I take my eyes off these quarters, this catapult of death, I'm done for, he thought, I'm finished, I'll die with the sight of Penson lying with his skull oozing its sense and memory out on horse's bedding. The dream-stupored and desperate eyes saw on the hunter's cool burnished croup the mark, raw as if only just branded on the flesh, of the horse's iron, the identical stamp they had found on Penson's face, with the hook of one heel jerked through the eyeball and the other heel caught in the palate's vertebrates. But when he felt their purpose advancing on him, he took his right hand out of his pocket for the first time and they saw the pistol in it.

"Don't touch the gate," he said, watching the horse's croup. "Don't touch it."

He did not shoot until Mrs. Lombe put her hand out to the latch, seeing or perhaps only divining the raising of her hand towards the box's gate, and then, without taking his eyes off the horse, he shot wildly out across them, the detonation splitting loud through the stable. The hauler's men and the huntsman ducked, but Mrs. Lombe did not stir but watched with clear stark eyes the blind horse as he whirled in his stall, spinning with forefeet slightly lifted, the tail arched and thrashing in panic across Candy's face and passing, and then the strong brutal head swinging across Candy's skull in its demented quest for sight.

"Come out, Candy," she whispered, but no one heard her. The hauler's men were out the door already and the huntsman was smoothing back his hair. "Come out, Candy," she said. "Come out."

He stood braced against the stall's side, the smoking pistol hanging in his fallen hand, his head pressed back against the board, the face small and fresh-looking, the eyes closed in an attitude of resigned and terrible waiting. He felt himself so, his body like something growing now to the wood and waiting, not for release any more in the gate's opening or Nancy's coming from the rapidly gyrating and seemingly illuminated wheels of fear, but release, as he swooned and drowned in terror, in the actual splinter of the complete and unalterably ordained end. But when he heard the huntsman's voice speaking again beyond the tide in which his body sank and perished, saying, "Let me by, Mrs. Lombe, let me by. This has got to be dealt with. This can't go on. Let me by"—he lifted the revolver again and again, but this time with his eyes closed fast against the vision of his own violent death, he fired out across the stable. And this time the horse shot upward, upright on its hocks, swung madly over him, and, whirling, smashed its heels savagely against the wooden gate. Mrs. Lombe's hand fell suddenly on Mr. Harrison's arm and her fingers clutched in anguish on his flesh, and they stood watching the horse spin, watched it fling itself from side to side in wild despair, while the little man lay pressed against the stall's side, his hands down, his head lifted, so far untouched and perhaps immuned by this passive, abeyant, this almost ludicrous posture of martyrdom.

They stood a while watching Candy pressed back against

the planks, his eyes closed, his right hand hanging with the pistol in it, and watched the horse quieting again and beginning to pace restlessly back and forth, its head swinging, pacing quickly, nervously back and forth across the straw with its head lifted and swinging and its nostrils quivering as they lipped the air for warning. Then Mrs. Lombe and the huntsman, as if the inaudible word had again been said, took up their positions at the open stable door. They did not speak much, only now and again a word about the weather, and at twenty past four Mrs. Lombe said in a low voice:

"There's Nancy. There's my daughter coming," and she went forward to meet her, neither the thoughts or the words ready yet, nor the emotion nameable that shook her heart.